WHITE EY[

On the rim, Clay hesitated to give the signal. It had been easy to pronounce judgment on the trappers when he hadn't set eyes on them. But now there they were: living, breathing human beings—white men like himself. Then he thought of his promise to the Apaches and how much taking his revenge on Miles Gillett meant to him. He waved the rifle once.

The poachers never had a prayer. The four Apaches swooped into the gully like ferocious birds of prey, pouncing on the startled trappers before they could bring a rifle or pistol into play.

And just like that it was over. The three trappers lay in spreading puddles of blood.

Clay walked to the bottom. He stood over one of the men and saw the trapper's eyes widen.

"Your eyes! They're blue!" the man said, then erupted in a coughing fit. "You're the one we heard about, aren't you? You're the White Apache!"

4

WHITE APACHE

QUICK
KILLER

Jake
McMasters

LEISURE BOOKS **NEW YORK CITY**

To Judy, Joshua, and Shane.

A LEISURE BOOK®

August 1994

Published by

Dorchester Publishing Co., Inc.
276 Fifth Avenue
New York, NY 10001

If you purchased this book without a cover you should be aware that this book is stolen property. It was reported as ''unsold and destroyed'' to the publisher and neither the author nor the publisher has received any payment for this ''stripped book.''

Copyright © 1994 by Dorchester Publishing Co., Inc.

All rights reserved. No part of this book may be reproduced or transmitted in any form or by any electronic or mechanical means, including photocopying, recording or by any information storage and retrieval system, without the written permission of the Publisher, except where permitted by law.

The name ''Leisure Books'' and the stylized ''L'' with design are trademarks of Dorchester Publishing Co., Inc.

Printed in the United States of America.

Prologue

His name was Chawn-clizzay and he was an Apache. In the language of his people the name meant "goat," and it certainly fit him this day as he scaled the high wall of a rocky gorge with the graceful ease and marvelous agility of a mountain goat. Overhead, the scorching summer sun blistered the arid Arizona landscape. The air was as still as death; not so much as a single leaf stirred anywhere.

Corded muscles rippling, Chawn-clizzay came to a wide shelf and stopped to check his back trail. He knew someone was back there, knew someone had been trailing him for half a day, yet he had not been able to catch more than one brief glimpse of the one shadowing him. And while Chawn-clizzay would never admit as much to another warrior, he had grown very worried.

Apaches were masters at moving stealthily and avoiding detection, able to rove the countryside without leaving a trace of their passing. It was said they were virtual ghosts, unseen and unheard until they cared to be. Like all men in his tribe, Chawn-clizzay had been schooled at a very early age in the art of being a living specter.

Yet now Chawn-clizzay's skill was doing him little good, and he could not understand why. When he first became aware of the man in the red headband, he had tried every trick he knew to shake the mysterious stalker. He had stuck to the rockiest, hardest ground, avoided skylines and open slopes, doubled back on himself several times, and more. To no avail. His pursuer had never lost the scent, never once been fooled. Of that he was certain.

What kind of man was he up against? Chawn-clizzay wondered as he scoured the jagged mouth of the gorge far below. He had no doubt the man had come to kill him for the bounty being offered by the white-eyes. Although he could not say exactly how he knew, he did.

Chawn-clizzay recalled his one glimpse, earlier that day, when he had stopped to quench his thirst. He had risen, wiped his mouth with his sleeve, and idly scanned the nearby rimrock. And there the man had been, brazenly standing in the open, his rifle glinting in the bright sunlight. Chawn-clizzay had been so surprised that he had gaped in disbelief until the lean figure in buckskins had melted into the shadows.

Many times over in the next several hours Chawn-clizzay had wondered why the man had done what he did, particularly when it would have been so easy for the stranger to pick him off from a distance. It was almost as if a challenge had been issued, as if the man wanted Chawn-clizzay to know he was being hunted so that he would have a fighting chance. But that was a ridiculous idea. No known enemy fought his people on their own terms because the Apaches won every time. They were the best at what they did, and justifiably proud of their prowess.

Chawn-clizzay's pondering was interrupted by a hint of motion several hundred yards away. Riveted to the cluster of boulders in question, he tucked his rifle to his shoulder and waited with a patience born of long practice for the hunter to show himself. Time dragged by, but the man in buckskins didn't appear.

Chawn-clizzay snorted like an angry buffalo, pivoted on his heel, and resumed scaling the wall. Presently he gained the top, and from this new vantage point he surveyed the gorge from end to end. No flash of red or brown gave the presence of the stalker away. He began to wonder if perhaps he wasn't behaving like a small child and letting his imagination play tricks on him. Or maybe he was simply mistaken. Most likely the stranger had gone elsewhere.

A barren switchback brought Chawn-clizzay to a tableland dominated by yucca. He broke into a tireless dogtrot so he could reach the Chiricahua Mountains that much sooner. As with most full-grown warriors, he was capable of covering seventy miles in a single day. Since he only had twenty miles to go to reach his destination, by nightfall he would be with his family. The thought brought a rare smile to his lips.

For over twenty minutes Chawn-clizzay ran eastward, until he detected movement out of the corner of his left eye. He looked around, expecting to see wrens or sparrows off in the brush. To his utter consternation, he saw the man in the red headband.

7

The stranger was over a hundred yards off, jogging on a parallel course. And he was staring right at Chawn-clizzay and grinning!

Chawn-clizzay broke stride and slowed, but only for an instant. Darting to the right, he plunged deeper into the yucca, weaving this way and that as openings presented themselves. When he had gone fifty feet he slanted to the left and crouched. Cocking his Winchester, he strained his ears to hear the telltale rustle of vegetation sure to give the stalker away. But all he heard was the faint whisper of the northwesterly breeze that had cropped up.

When half-an-hour had gone by and nothing happened, Chawn-clizzay bore to the south in a wide loop that would bring him out on the east side of the tableland. He was more troubled now than ever. The man in buckskins seemed to be playing some sort of strange game with him. Even worse, the man seemed to be his equal at woodcraft, for somehow the stranger had been able to scale the gorge and keep up with him without being detected.

Chawn-clizzay wondered if his pursuer were an Apache. He hadn't gotten a close enough look to see the man's features, but he had noticed the man's hair, which was cut short instead of being allowed to grow to the shoulders, or longer, as was Apache custom.

A clearing appeared. Chawn-clizzay mistakenly went straight across it rather than going around. He was halfway to the other side when he belatedly registered a hawkish form poised among the yucca to the north. Spinning, he brought his rifle to bear, but he did not yet have the gun level when thunder peeled and an invisible hammer slammed into his chest. Dimly, he felt himself hit the ground. There was a ticklish sensation as blood gushed from the wound, splattering on his neck. He tried to rise but his body refused to obey his mental commands.

Suddenly the man wearing the red cloth head-band loomed above him. Chawn-clizzay saw a stern, almost cruel face, half-white, half-Indian. The dark eyes fixed on his were as cold as ice.

"You were careless, Chawn-clizzay," the man spoke in flawless Apache. "You should have known they would send me sooner or later."

Chawn-clizzay licked his unexpectedly dry lips and forced his mouth to move. "Who—?"

"*Tats-ah-das-ay-go.*"

At last all was clear. Chawn-clizzay thought of his devoted wife and young son and prayed *Yusn* would grant him the strength to draw his knife and thrust. Just once was all it would take. He attempted to move his hand and had to choke back intense frustration when his arm wouldn't budge. Moments later his suffering was cut short by an inky veil that enveloped his mind. The last sight he beheld was the killer's countenance creasing in the same grin as before, only now he realized it wasn't a grin, after all. It was a smug, triumphant smirk.

Then everything went black.

Chapter One

About the same time that the Apache named Chawn-clizzay breathed his last, another man was taking a deep breath to fill his lungs with air. Clay Taggart stood perched on a flat boulder on the bank of a narrow stream situated high in the remote, rugged Chiricahuas. Below him the stream widened into a murky pool not quite five feet deep.

Taggart stepped to the edge of the boulder, extended his arms, and dived. Cool water encased him in a velvety cocoon, all the more welcome because it afforded great relief from the burning sun. As his fingers brushed the muddy bottom, he arched his spine and whipped upward, cleaving the surface smoothly. Exhaling, he tread water and allowed himself to relax.

This was the first dip Taggart had taken in months, ever since a fluke of fate had resulted in his being taken in by a band of renegade Chiricahua Apaches.

Quick Killer

The *Shis-Inday*, they called themselves. The men of the woods. And now, should any of his old acquaintances see him, they would rightfully think he had gone Injun, as the saying went.

Taggart's dark hair was worn Apache style and hung to his shoulders in a shaggy mane. His skin had been bronzed a coppery hue, the soles of his feet coated with callouses. Except for his striking lake-blue eyes, he was the perfect picture of a robust, full-blooded Apache. And of late he had even begun to think like one, which bothered Taggart immensely.

Mere months ago, he had been a moderately successful rancher living not far from Tucson. Today, he was hiding out on the vast Chiricahua reservation, a wanted man, sought by the army and civilian authorities alike, despised by whites and most Apaches. How, he wondered, could so much have gone so wrong so rapidly?

The answer was as plain as the nose on Clay's face: Miles Gillett. It was the wealthy rancher who had seen fit to frame Clay in order to get his greedy hands on Clay's ranch. It was Gillett who had to shoulder the blame for the lynch party that left Clay for dead. And it was Gillett who was indirectly accountable for the bloody revenge Clay had taken on those who nearly hung him.

Suddenly, Clay had the feeling he wasn't alone. Swiveling in the water, he scoured both banks. Months ago he wouldn't have spied a thing out of the ordinary. But the many weeks he'd spent among the *Shis-Inday* had sharpened his senses to the point where he immediately saw the vague outline of a man crouched in the high grass. Acting as if he hadn't noticed, he swam leisurely to shore, to the strip of gravel where he had left his clothes and weapons.

Clay casually wiped his hands on grass and reached for his breechcloth. But instead of picking it up, he snatched his Winchester and took a running dive into the grass, rolling and flattening on his stomach as he landed. He leveled the rifle and worked the lever to feed a new cartridge into the chamber.

Fifteen yards off, the man abruptly stood. He was a handsome Apache with the weathered features typical of his kind, a rifle clasped in the crook of his left elbow. He made no move to employ the gun. Instead, he raised his other arm in greeting and said a single word, *"Nejeunee."*

Clay slowly stood and eased the hammer down on his Winchester. "Friend," he said in response. His Apache was far from perfect, but he had the satisfaction of knowing he spoke it better than most other whites and was improving all the time. "I am pleased to see you, Cuchillo Negro. It has been seven sleeps since any of you have so much as spoken to me."

The Apache came forward, his inscrutable visage providing no clues as to the reason for his unforeseen visit. "It is time we talked, Lickoyee-shis-inday."

White Apache. The name had been bestowed on Clay by another warrior, the one responsible for saving him from the lynch party, a man Clay had assumed was a staunch friend until recently. "I will gladly hear your words. Wait a moment," he responded. In no time, he donned his breechcloth, shirt, and knee-high moccasins. Around his waist he strapped a pair of matching Colts in twin holsters. From the back of one dangled a large butcher knife. Twin bandoleers crisscrossed his chest. "Now I am ready."

Quick Killer

Cuchillo Negro stepped to a majestic willow and sat with his back to the wide trunk. Had Clay Taggart been able to peer into the warrior's mind, he would have been amazed to find that Cuchillo Negro was greatly concerned about his welfare. The two of them had never been all that close, so it would have interested Clay greatly to learn that Cuchillo Negro thought quite highly of him, but for a reason Clay would never have suspected.

Cuchillo Negro stared at Clay as he took a seat, then the warrior picked his statements carefully. "We have hunted together, skinned the same deer together."

"This is true," Clay acknowledged. He knew enough of Apache ways to realize that something of the utmost importance had brought the warrior to him, and he was eager to learn its nature. Ever since the band had returned from their last raid, the four warriors had virtually shunned him. Their cold attitude had bothered him initially, until he concluded they were upset because a fifth warrior, Amarillo, had been slain fighting his enemies.

"We drank from the same spring, slept beside the same fire."

"This too is true."

"Never once have I spoken in anger to you, like Fiero. Never once have I tried to make you follow my path instead of your own, like Delgadito."

"True," Clay said, while inwardly he filed the reference to Delgadito away for future consideration.

"So would you say we are brothers, White Apache?"

The question confused Clay. Given the history of the *Shis-Inday*, it was rare for them to regard outsiders as brothers. They had fought the Spanish when the Spaniards first came to the New World.

13

They had raided into Mexico as the whim moved them. They had resisted the influx of whites into their domain and lost a costly clash with the United States. To top it all off, they were even in a state of perpetual war with most other tribes.

Clay had spent months in the company of the renegade band that had saved him, and he'd gotten to know the five stalwart warriors fairly well. For the most part, the Apaches had never been more friendly than they had to be, the lone exception being Delgadito, the former leader who had lost his right to lead when his band was slaughtered by scalp hunters.

As for the others, there was Fiero, the firebrand who lusted for war as some men lusted for women. The youngest was Ponce, so eager to make his mark according to the time-honored Apache ways of stealing and killing. The fourth had been Amarillo. And here sat the fifth, Cuchillo Negro, the one who always held his own council, the one who spoke the least but whose influence always held great weight, the one who had always seemed so aloof. Yet he referred to Clay as he would his best friend.

To Clay, it made no sense. But he answered, "Yes, I would say we are brothers. After all we have been through together."

"Brothers listen to brothers," Cuchillo Negro said. Then he did an odd thing. He tilted his head and glanced upward. "Do you see the high limbs being rustled by the breeze?"

"Yes," Clay said.

"So can I. Yet we cannot see the breeze itself. No man can." Cuchillo Negro paused. "The thoughts of men are much like the wind. We can see the actions that come about as a result of thoughts, but we cannot see the thoughts themselves. Would you agree?"

Completely puzzled, Clay replied, "As always, you speak with a straight tongue."

"Sometimes the wind is so strong that it pushes against us, trying to move us against our will. Has this ever happened to you, Lickoyee-shis-inday?"

"Sometimes," Clay admitted. He figured the warrior would elaborate but Cuchillo Negro sat gazing at the treetops for the next couple of minutes, his knit brow indicating he was lost in reflection. Clay would have liked to quiz him at length but that wasn't the Apache way. Men spoke their peace at their own pace. To pry was to court their anger.

While the custom frequently bothered Clay, he admired the Apaches for their laconic natures. It was a welcome change from white society. There were no snoops or busybodies to contend with, no town gossips who had nothing better to do with their lives than spread the latest malicious rumors concerning people they hardly knew. In the Apache scheme of things, everyone was expected to mind their own business.

Cuchillo Negro cleared his throat. Unknown to Clay Taggart, inwardly he was in great turmoil. Meddling in the affairs of two others was strictly taboo, yet he couldn't bring himself to sit back and do nothing while the white-eye was being manipulated by Delgadito. Since White Apache had been accepted into the band, and had risked his life on their behalf on more than one occasion, Cuchillo Negro felt it only right that the white man be treated with the respect due all, not as a puppet in another's quest for power and prestige. But he had to be careful. He risked antagonizing Delgadito. Cuchillo Negro knew he had already overstepped the line that separated friendly advice from intentional meddling. Delgadito would be entirely justified in challenging him to formal, ritual combat if he found out. "Have you ever noticed that sometimes branches are broken by strong wind?"

"Yes," Clay said, at a loss to know how the remark applied to him. He was taken aback when the warrior abruptly rose.

"Take care, Lickoyee-shis-inday that the wind does not break you." Cuchillo Negro turned and walked off, and soon he was lost among the cottonwoods.

Frowning, Clay stood and hiked westward. This made twice that Cuchillo Negro had implied he couldn't trust Delgadito. The first time he had dismissed the notion as preposterous. After all, it had been Delgadito who saved him from being hung, Delgadito who later had gone to great lengths to safeguard his life. Surely, he had reasoned, Delgadito wouldn't have invested so much time and energy in his welfare unless Delgadito genuinely cared.

But now Clay wasn't so certain. Delgadito hadn't been quite as friendly during the week or so leading up to Amarillo's death. And since then Delgadito had wanted nothing to do with him, hardly the act of a staunch friend. Perhaps Cuchillo Negro had been right all along. Perhaps Delgadito had used him as some sort of puppet to suit a purpose Clay had yet to divine.

A flock of sparrows winged from a thicket on Clay's left, breaking his concentration. He passed on by and crossed a wide meadow. Several grazing horses glanced at him, then resumed eating.

After the last raid the Apaches hadn't returned to Warm Springs, the sanctuary they usually used, but to another isolated retreat hidden high in the Chiricahuas. Sweet Grass, they called it, because of the abundant forage to be found. The warriors had set up camp in a sheltered nook at the base of a

Quick Killer

high cliff. Clay had stayed with them the first week, until their cold treatment influenced him to seek a spot elsewhere. On a bench that straddled the lower slope of a mountain he'd found a suitable spot.

Several times during his climb Clay paused to survey the valley. Bathed in sunshine, the green of the verdant vegetation and the blue of the sinuous stream lent the scene the aspect of a literal Eden. Over half-a-mile away, a few stray tendrils of smoke wafted skyward.

Clay came to the bench and walked to his lean-to. He knelt, opened a pouch, and removed a couple of strips of venison jerky he had made himself. As he munched, he dwelled on the same problem that had confronted him for days, the issue of what to do next. Should he stay among the Apaches where he clearly wasn't wanted, or should he leave the territory for parts unknown? Venturing to Tucson or any of his other old haunts was akin to committing suicide since he was wanted by both the U.S. Army and the civil authorities. To complicate matters, a large bounty had been put on his head, dead or alive, a certain lure for every bounty hunter and money-hungry kid west of the Pecos.

Clay had always been a loner, always kept pretty much to himself, but he'd never figured on ending his days a complete outcast. He had a few close friends, a very few. He'd very much like to see them again, but he dared not. Once he traveled beyond the boundaries of the reservation, his life wouldn't be worth a plugged nickel. Not that it was worth any more in the reservation. He'd already made an enemy of Palacio, an influential warrior, and he wouldn't be at all surprised if Palacio sent someone to rub him out.

As if on cue, a jay higher on the mountain squawked in alarm. It was the kind of cry jays only voiced when they were extremely upset, either by the presence of a roving predator or intruding humans. And all the members of the band were down in the valley.

Clay cocked his head and listened intently. There might be a bear or mountain lion abroad, or perhaps even a rare jaguar. Delgadito had told him that many years ago jaguars were quite numerous in the Chiricahuas, but the spotted cats had almost died out shortly after the coming of the Spaniards.

Finishing his first piece of jerky, Clay went to bite into another when a squirrel erupted in a fit of irate chattering, in about the same vicinity as the jay. His curiosity was aroused. Stuffing the jerky back in the pouch, he grabbed his Winchester and padded into the ponderosa pines. The carpet of yielding needles underneath enabled him to move as silently as his shadow.

There had been a time when Clay Taggart wouldn't have bothered investigating. Back in his ranching days he had paid little attention to the cries of wild animals. Where Nature was concerned, he had been like a babe in the woods. Ironically, though, he'd always assumed he knew just about all there was to know about wilderness survival. Fortunately, his stint with the Apaches had disabused him of such idiocy.

To fully understand the ways of the wild, a person had to live in the wild. To fully appreciate the rhythms of the wildlife, a person had to experience those rhythms firsthand. The Apaches were adept at living off the land because in a sense they were as much a part of the land as the animals they shared the land with. They were at home in the mountains, on the plains, or in the deserts. The land was in their blood, one might say.

The same could not be said to an equal degree of Clay Taggart, but he had learned a whole new appreciation for Nature and had learned to relate to the multitude of creatures inhabiting Nature's domains. They were no longer simply dumb brutes put on Earth for humankind to exterminate at will. They lived, they breathed, they did things for a reason. Just as the jay and the squirrel must have done.

Both had fallen silent, so Clay had no means of pinpointing their exact locations. He slowed, searching the slopes above. If he saw a mountain lion, he'd take a shot. Apaches were especially fond of lion meat. A fresh kill would make a dandy gift to offer Delgadito and the others in the hope of mending fences. But if he saw a bear, he wouldn't fire unless his life was in peril. Apaches had high regard for bears, something Clay had learned only after coming to live among them. Bears were their wise brothers, as they put it, and no Apache would ever eat the flesh of a brother.

The forest was quiet, unnaturally so. There should be birds singing, insects buzzing, the chattering of chipmunks and squirrels. The silence had an ominous feel about it, like the lull before a storm.

Clay halted beside a pine and squatted. As Delgadito had taught him, he gazed through the brush at knee level, where the moving legs of large animals and men would be most obvious. Though he looked and looked, he saw nothing other than undergrowth.

As the minutes dragged by and nothing happened, Clay decided that whatever had agitated the wildlife had probably drifted elsewhere. He stood and turned, then realized the forest continued to be as still as a tomb.

Seconds later, the faint snap of a twig reached Clay's ears. Promptly ducking low, he moved warily in the direction the sound came from, diligently placing his feet with consummate care. He held the Winchester low to the ground so stray shafts of sunlight wouldn't glint off the metal and give him away.

Clay went forty yards without finding whatever had busted the twig. It could have been a deer, even a raccoon, but his gut instinct told him otherwise. He veered to the right, past a patch of briars. Suddenly, a section rustled. Automatically, he brought the rifle to bear, but held his fire when a rabbit hopped into the open. The second it saw him, it bounded off in prodigious leaps, making enough noise to alert every predator within hundreds of feet.

Clay dashed to a patch of scrub brush and flattened. Doing as he'd been instructed by Delgadito, he quickly covered as much of himself as he could with fallen limbs and leaves so that he would blend in with the background. Then he laid motionless, awaiting developments.

Less than a minute elapsed when something moved deep in the woods. A stocky form flitted across the ground toward the briars, halting among a packed growth of ponderosas a dozen yards away, where it vanished as if sucked down into the very earth.

Clay wasn't fooled. Moving only his eyes, he probed the forest for others, and when none appeared he focused on the strip of ground between the briars and the ponderosas, certain that was where the man would show himself again. Even though he knew it would happen, he was surprised when the heavily built Indian sprang up like a sprouting plant not eight feet from his hiding place.

It was an Apache, but one Clay had never seen before. The newcomer wore buckskin leggings and high moccasins. His chest was like that of a bronze sculpture, his sinews rippling as he moved. The man sniffed the air, then bent to see into the depth of the briars. Satisfied no one lurked within, the warrior straightened, put a hand to his lips, and twittered in perfect imitation of a mountain bluebird, a series of *terr-terr-terr* cries that would have fooled Clay into thinking they were the genuine article had Clay not seen the man make them.

Two more Apaches popped up from out of nowhere. One was skinny, a jagged scar on the left side of his chest. The other wore a faded blue army jacket with a torn sleeve. All three converged and huddled to consult in whispers.

Clay caught just a few snatches of meaningless words. The warrior sporting the scar glanced in his direction and he involuntarily tensed, dreading discovery. The last time he'd encountered an unknown Apache, the man had tried to kill him. But there was no outcry. The warrior's gaze drifted beyond him and around to the north.

At a gesture from the Apache wearing the jacket, the three men jogged off down the slope.

To ensure he wasn't spotted, Clay stayed put until they were out of sight. Rising, he hastened in their wake, anxious to learn the reason they were there. His best guess was that they were friends of the warriors in Delgadito's band. Yet, if that were the case, why were they sneaking into the valley instead of entering through the gap to the south? Had they been sent by Palacio to dispose of him?

Caution kept Clay a prudent distance back. Occasionally, he glimpsed the three Apaches as they glided downward. They came to the bench and right away saw the lean-to. He crept to a weed choked knob that afforded a clear view and watched them rummage through his meager belongings. The stocky one had the audacity to take a stick of his jerky.

Downward the trio went, to the edge of the meadow. Rather than cross, they went around, and Clay observed them test the breeze to guarantee they stayed downwind of the horses. They were leaving nothing to chance.

Clay became more troubled the farther the three warriors went. Friends of Delgadito's would hardly need to employ the degree of stealth being exercised by the newcomers. But maybe, he reflected, they weren't sure Delgadito was there so they were exercising typical Apache vigilance.

The warrior in the blue shirt took the lead. They slowed to a cat-walk shortly thereafter, spreading out as they drew within sight of the cliff.

Clay hung back, in a quandary over the right thing to do. He could fire a few shots to alert Delgadito, or he could bide his time and avoid making a fool of himself should the trio prove friendly. He choose the latter.

All four members of the renegade band were in camp. A low fire blazed, the wood crackling loud enough to be heard in the surrounding trees. Delgadito, Fiero, and Ponce were gambling with a deck of cards stolen from a ranch the band had raided several months ago, while Cuchillo Negro looked on without much interest.

Clay saw the three new Apaches lower themselves to the ground and crawl. His brain shrieked a strident warning that they must be enemies, but once again logic intervened and he persuaded himself the trio had indeed been sent by Palacio and were seeking him. Naturally, they wouldn't show themselves until they found their quarry.

Thus convinced, Clay didn't interfere when the one in the blue coat stopped behind a bush and parted the branches. He didn't move a muscle when the warrior poked a rifle through the opening. But when he saw the man take a steady bead on Delgadito and touch a thumb to the hammer, he knew beyond a shadow of a doubt that his first hunch had been the right one and the three newcomers were up to no good. Unfortunately, he had no time to fire warning shots, no time to do anything other than what he did; namely, to rear erect and charge the warrior about to fire.

Chapter Two

He came down out of Apache Pass with a pack animal in tow and made for Fort Bowie using the Tucson-Mesilla road. Clad in buckskins, his short hair crowned by a red headband, he was little different in appearance from the many friendly Indians and breeds who used the road on a regular basis. But there was something about this man that drew uneasy looks from other travelers and compelled those in his path to move quickly aside to grant him passage. Perhaps his sharply hawkish features were to blame, or his hard as flint eyes, or maybe the latent suggestion of a severely cruel disposition that shrouded him like a dark cloud.

Tats-ah-das-ay-go made no attempt to hide his disdain for those who moved out of his way. To his way of thinking, they were all weak and worthless, little better than human sheep who quaked at the presence of a wolf in their midst. Even the white-eyes gave him a wide berth, confirming his belief in his own superiority.

Most of those Tats-ah-das-ay-go passed noticed the burden his pack animal carried and flinched at the sight. A few crossed themselves or muttered hasty prayers.

Tats-ah-das-ay-go knew they were afraid and was pleased. He liked nothing better than to inspire terror since it served to enhance his reputation, which in turn made his job easier in the long run. By nightfall, news of his latest success would have spread far and wide, and when he went into town people would point at him behind his back and whisper to one another.

As well they should. Tats-ah-das-ay-go was proud of his accomplishment. He was the best there was at what he did, as the fourteen renegades rotting in the ground confirmed. Not for nothing was he the highest paid scout, tracker and hunter in all of Arizona.

A dust cloud rose in the far distance. Tats-ah-das-ay-go's dark eyes narrowed, reading details few others could. He knew it was a cavalry patrol long before the patrol spotted him. When the officer at the head of the column raised a gloved hand to halt the soldiers, Tats-ah-das-ay-go reined up.

"Hello, Quick Killer," said Captain Gerald Forester, a tough veteran of the Apache campaigns and one of the few officers who bothered to give the Fifth Cavalry scouts the time of day.

Quick Killer gave a curt nod.

"Is that who I think it is?" the officer asked.

"Chawn-clizzay."

"He give you any trouble?"

"You joke, white-eye," Quick Killer said indignantly. "None are as good as Tats-ah-das-ay-go. They are all easy."

"Including Delgadito?" Captain Forester responded, and grinned when the halfbreed flashed crimson
with anger. It was common knowledge around the
fort that twice Quick Killer had gone after Delgadito
and each time returned empty-handed.

"His luck cannot hold out forever. I will get him
one day. *Shee-dah*."

"Then you'd better hurry," Captain Forester said,
"or Nah-kah-yen will beat you to it."

Quick Killer was suddenly all interest. "What do
you say?"

"Haven't you heard? Colonel Reynolds gave permission for Nah-kah-yen and two other scouts to
hunt Delgadito's band down. They left the fort
pretty near a week ago and headed deep into
the Chiricahuas. Nah-kah-yen has probably lifted
Delgadito's hair by now."

Raw resentment ate at Quick Killer's innards like
a scorching acid. Nah-kah-yen was the only scout
whose record came anywhere near matching his,
and an abiding rivalry had sprung up between the
two of them. Each was determined to outshine the
other. Should Nah-kah-yen bring Delgadito to bay,
it would diminish Quick Killer's standing tremen-
dously.

"Nah-kah-yen *no vale nada*," he spat without
thinking.

"That's your opinion," Captain Forester said. "The
colonel thinks right highly of him."

"Nah-kah-yen will fail," Quick Killer said, but his
tone lacked confidence. For all his dislike of the
Tonto, and despite what he said in public, he had
to admit that Nah-kah-yen was extremely skilled. "If
anyone brings in Delgadito, it will be me."

The officer removed his hat to brush dust from
the brim. "Maybe it will. Nah-kah-yen might have

bitten off more than he can chew this time around."

"I do not follow your trail."

"Haven't you heard? Word had drifted down from the Adjutant General's office that the turncoat we're after, the one called the White Apache, is riding with Delgadito. The two of them combined could be more than Nah-kah-yen can handle." Forester jammed the hat back on. "Well, enough dawdling. I have a patrol to make." He waved his arm and led his troops westward at a trot.

Quick Killer rode off, breathing shallow so as not to inhale the choking dust. Once clear of the cloud he swiftly brought his bay to a gallop, motivated by a sudden eagerness to have a talk with the colonel. He didn't slow down until the hill on which the fort was located hove into view.

The sentries and gate guards knew Quick Killer on sight so he was admitted without a fuss. He rode straight to the hitching post in front of the post headquarters. As he looped the reins, the door opened and out strode a burly sergeant whose bristly mustache seemed to stretch from ear to ear.

"Well, well, well. If it ain't the high and mighty Quick Killer," Sergeant Joe McKinn said. "Didn't expect you back for another week or better. Chawn-clizzay must not have put up much of a scrap."

Quick Killer made no reply. He was not one to accord respect to those who showed him none, and he had a particular dislike for the sergeant who took advantage of every occasion to insult him. He stepped toward the doorway but the noncom barred his path.

"Where do you reckon you're going, scout?"

"I must talk to colonel."

"Do you have an appointment? Reynolds is a busy man. We can't be interrupting his work every time someone gets a hair to stop on by. Especially breeds."

The sergeant would never know how close he came to having his throat slit. Quick Killer's hand started to drift toward the hilt of his knife, but he stopped himself in time. To give in to his fury would result in his being branded a renegade, just like those he hunted for a living. The shame would be almost more than he could bear. "I must see colonel," he insisted.

"Run along and get drunk on *tiswin*. I'll pass on the word and let you know when he's free."

"I must," Quick Killer said. He went to go around but McKinn grabbed the front of his shirt.

"Didn't you hear me, breed? I told you to get lost."

Again Quick Killer's anger nearly got the better of him. He was on the verge of lashing out when a stern voice intruded from within the building.

"What the hell is the meaning of this, Sergeant? Release that man this instant."

McKinn let go and snapped to attention as a young officer appeared. A recent arrival to the fort and fresh out of the academy, Lieutenant James Petersen clasped his hands behind his rigid back and gave the noncom a withering look. "Correct me if I'm in error, Sergeant, but isn't this man one of our regular scouts?"

"Yes, sir," McKinn growled.

"Which means he's on the army's payroll, the same as we are. Which puts him on the same side as us, doesn't it?"

"Yes, sir," McKinn answered. He wanted to plant a boot on his own backside for not remembering the junior officer had been conversing with the orderly moments ago. In his estimation, Petersen was too damn green to be serving a hitch on the frontier. The man knew virtually nothing about Indians, and even less about Apaches and breeds.

"Then kindly explain to me why you felt it necessary to treat him the way you did?" Petersen demanded. As the newest officer at the post, he had been looking for a chance to put the arrogant know-it-all noncom in his place and this was the perfect opportunity. "It's hard enough, I understand, to enlist Apaches willing to fight against their own kind, without you scaring them off."

"There's more to it than that, sir," McKinn stubbornly held his ground. "If we don't put these bastards in their place, they get all uppity on us."

Petersen smiled smugly. "I had no idea you were such an expert on Indian affairs. Maybe I should contact the War Department and advise them to consult with you before making future decisions." He dismissed the sergeant with a wave. "Run along, mister, before I have you up on report. Unless, of course, you'd rather go on giving me guff and spend the rest of the day jogging around the parade ground while carrying a fifty-pound rock."

Quick Killer did not let his delight at the noncom's comeuppance show. He watched McKinn huff off, then straightened to impress the junior officer and said in his best English, "Please, sir. It is very important I speak to the colonel."

Lieutenant Petersen had been about to return indoors. The cause of the disturbance had not been all that important to him except as a means to teach the sergeant a lesson. Now he regarded the man before him with a mixture of curiosity and scarcely suppressed contempt. For all his talk about the need to treat the scouts decently, secretly he rated them as akin to intelligent animals trained to perform on command. "Does it involve a matter of life and death?" he asked, half sarcastically.

The scout took him literally. "Yes, sir."

"It does?" Petersen scratched his smooth chin, then motioned. "Come on in, then, and I'll see if the colonel will talk to you."

At Quick Killer's entrance the orderly behind the desk gave a start and commenced to rise out of his chair.

"At ease, Private," Petersen said. "I'll handle this."

The door to the office stood ajar. The lieutenant knocked, was bid to enter, and went in. Quick Killer heard the gruff voice of the commanding white-eye raised in irritation. He paid no attention to the gawking orderly but stood as if carved from wood.

"All right, you can go in," Petersen said on reappearing, and lowered his voice. "But don't take much of the colonel's valuable time. He has important duties to attend to."

How well Quick Killer recalled Reynold's white hair and mustache, a rarity among whites and Indians. Knowing that the white-eyes were fond of puffing out their chests and squaring their shoulders whenever they were in the colonel's presence, he did the same. "Thank you for seeing me," he said.

"Quick Killer, isn't it?" Reynolds said, setting down the ink pen he had been writing with. "I remember you from that wagon train business. Horrible, truly horrible."

Quick Killer recalled the eight Mexican traders who had been found the previous year. They had been on their way to Tucson from Chihuahua when they were ambushed in Coyote Canyon, very near the fort. The Apaches had been in such a hurry to take their plunder and leave that they hadn't bothered to mutilate their victims as they ordinarily did.

Quick Killer

Instead they had hung the Mexicans upside down over roaring fires. The stench had been awful, but Quick Killer would hardly call the deaths horrible compared to some he had seen.

"What can I do for you?" Colonel Reynolds asked.

"I learn you send Nah-kah-yen or Keen Sighted as you call him, after Delgadito."

Reynolds propped both elbows on his desk and cupped his hands. "It was Captain Parmalee who submitted the request. All I did was concur with his proposal. Why? How does this pertain to you?"

Quick Killer hid his annoyance at the revelation. He should have suspected that it had been Parmalee, since Parmalee always had liked Nah-kah-yen better. All fourteen scouts had learned to accept the favoritism as a fact of life, but it still galled him. "I want to kill Delgadito myself."

The colonel blinked, glanced at the lieutenant, and cleared his throat. "You know as well as I do that Captain Parmalee is in charge of the scouts. If you have a complaint, I suggest you take it up with him."

Quick Killer thought fast. "I come to you because men say you fair with Indian. Men say you can be trusted." He paused, disliking the need to act like a cur begging for food at the feet of its master but seeing no other way to get his heart's desire. "You know Delgadito is worst renegade of all. You know how many he has killed. It is time someone stop him. And I am the one."

"I have been kept informed of your outstanding record," Colonel Reynolds said, "and I dare say no one is better qualified to hunt Delgadito down. But I also recollect that you went after him before and failed to bring him in."

"I will this time," Quick Killer vowed.

"Maybe so. But, as I've stressed, it's not my place to decide. There is such a thing as a chain of command in the U.S. Army. I realize it's not a concept you can comprehend, but it means you must go to Captain Parmalee first and he will relay any pertinent requests to me. The disposition of the scouts is in his hands. You'll have to talk to him if you think you're being treated unfairly."

Severely disappointed, Quick Killer said, "He not listen."

"Do you want to file a formal complaint?" the colonel asked impatiently.

"No," Quick Killer said, knowing it would be a waste of his time.

"Fine. Is there anything else?"

"No." Rotating on a heel, Quick Killer left before his simmering resentment showed. He had been stupid to expect fair treatment from the white-eyes. They looked down their noses on all who were not of their race, on Mexicans and Indians and blacks, but most especially on those of mixed ancestry like himself. The only thing that could be said in their favor was that they were no different from those they despised. Mexicans and Indians and blacks also looked down on his kind.

It was a heavy burden for any set of shoulders to bear, and Quick Killer had been doing so for twenty-nine years. He had been constantly mistreated from the day he was old enough to stand until the day he killed for the very first time. And what a glorious day that had been! Just thinking about it sent a tingle of excitement coursing down his spine, for slaying that Navaho had taught Quick Killer a remarkable truth that had served him in good stead ever since: People treated those whom they feared with respect. Not genuine respect born of high esteem, but respect bred by the very oldest of human instincts, self-preservation. He had discovered that those who formerly poked fun at him tread lightly if they believed their lives might be forfeit if they did not. How sweet life had become! he reflected. On the day that Navaho died, he had been reborn.

"Hey, buck! Are you fixing to grow roots there, or can I mosey on by?"

Quick Killer glanced up at the gruff hail and was annoyed to find he had blundered into the middle of the rutted track the wagons took from the sutler's store to the gate. The muleskinner bellowing at him was an older man he knew but whose name he couldn't remember. He moved out of the way and the wagon rattled on by.

Swiftly, Quick Killer made his way to the small building housing the office of the Chief of Scouts, as the army styled their liaison with the warriors who had volunteered to so serve. Parmalee insisted that all his scouts knock before entering, but this day Quick Killer didn't bother.

The captain was caught by surprise. He sat in his chair, his feet propped on his desk, a half-empty flask tipped to his lips. As the door swung wide, he hastily lowered the bottle out of sight and swung his feet to the floor. "What the hell!" he blurted. "What do you think you're doing, barging in here like this?"

Quick Killer halted in front of the desk and shifted his rifle from his left hand to his right. He did not rant and rave as whites would have done. He simply stared.

"Tats-ah-das-ay-go," Captain Vincent Parmalee said, slightly slurring the syllables. He had taken the time to learn the Indian names of all the scouts, not because he cared a damn about them, but because the army claimed it was a means of establishing a working rapport. Had it been Parmalee's choice, he would have had nothing to do with the lot of them. To him, they were filthy, ignorant savages, hardly better than the renegades they hunted.

Parmalee resented them not only for who and what they were, but because he had been picked against his will to serve as the officer in charge. He had objected strenuously, to no avail. None other than General George Cook himself had decided that it took an Apache to catch an Apache. And Colonel Reynolds, in implementing the program, had chosen the only officer who had ever spent any time among them. It had been Parmalee's misfortune to have spent several months prior to his enlistment working on a boundary commission that had dealings with the Mimbres. He'd pointed out to the colonel that he had hardly spoken three words to an Apache the entire time, but that hadn't mattered. Reynolds had made his choice, and the decision had been final.

Now Parmalee looked into the smoldering eyes of the one scout he secretly feared and put on a blustery front. "The next time you want to see me, Tats-ah-das-ay-go, by damn you'd better show some courtesy and knock first. You wouldn't want me entering your lodge without permission, would you?"

Quick Killer stayed silent, his contempt knowing no bounds. He could practically smell the white-eye's fright, and it insulted him to think that he had to work under such a weakling.

Parmalee licked his thin lips, then casually jammed the cork back into his flask and slid the whiskey into a drawer. "Now that we've settled your rudeness, would you mind telling me what the devil has you in such high dudgeon?" He paused, gazing through the doorway at the headquarters building. "Oh. I see. You've brought back Chawn-clizzay already. You're to be commended for a job well done."

"Not job I want," Quick Killer said.

"Oh?" Parmalee had regained his composure and assumed the superior air he always put on around the scouts. "Now I get it. You've heard about Nah-kah-yen."

"I should go after Delgadito. Not him."

"As I recollect, you had your chance and failed."

"Delgadito not like other Apaches. He much smarter, clever like a fox."

"Smarter than you, at any rate," Captain Parmalee said. "But just so you'll know, all things being equal, I doubt Nah-kah-yen will do much better than you did. But he has an edge."

"Edge?"

"Yep. He's been wanting to go after Delgadito for months, but I kept putting him off, telling him that he'd be wasting a lot of effort for nothing. The Chiricahua and Dragoon mountains cover a hell of a lot of territory. It'd be like looking for a needle in a haystack." He hooked his fingers behind his head. "But Nah-kah-yen is a persistent cuss. He came up with a brainstorm that might enable him to do what no else has done."

"What is brainstorm?" Quick Killer wanted to know.

"An idea. A bright idea." Parmalee chuckled. "Since Nah-kah-yen knew he couldn't get at Delgadito directly, he started nosing around the reservation, trying to find out who else was in the band. At first no one would give him the time of day, but then someone let it slip that a young buck named Ponce is one of those who rides with

Delgadito. Later, Nah-kah-yen learned that Ponce is partial to sneaking into one of the villages now and then to see his sweetheart."

Quick Killer's face didn't show the shame he felt at not having thought of the idea before his rival. He had taken it for granted that no one would turn the renegades in and never made the attempt.

"So how could I refuse when Nah-kah-yen asked me for permission to go after the band? It's the best lead we've had in years. We might even be able to kill two birds with one stone."

"The White Apache?"

"You've heard, have you?" Parmalee nodded. "Yet another reason for me to let Nah-kah-yen have a try. Command has made a priority out of this Taggart character. They want him, want him badly. More than they want Delgadito."

Here was information of some consequence and Quick Killer filed it for future consideration. "That why they pay large bounty?"

"You're learning. It'll be quite a feather in Nah-kah-yen's cap if he kills both Delgadito and Clay Taggart." Parmalee began sorting through a stack of papers. "As for you, I have another job you might like."

"I want Delgadito and this Lickoyee-shis-inday."

"We've just been all through that," Parmalee said irritably. He pulled out a sheet and studied it. "Here's the man I want you to try to find. His name is Chipota—"

"The Lipan," Quick Killer said with a measure of disgust.

"Don't sound so put out. He's been raiding for four months now, and he recently stole a shipment of flour and other foodstuffs bound for Fort Grant."

"I not become scout to fight men who steal food

for families," Quick Killer protested.

"You don't have the luxury of choosing who you go after and who you don't," Captain Parmalee reminded him. "Technically, we're not even supposed to let you kill these renegades. That should be our job. But it's a hell of a sight better all around if we give you boys a free reign. You get the job done with a minimum of fuss and everyone's happy." He set the paper aside. "Just so the Eastern press doesn't find out. Those damned bleeding heart journalists would have a field day at our expense."

Quick Killer turned and walked to the entrance, stopping when the officer said his name.

"One more thing. I don't want you getting any notions about going after Delgadito yourself. So help me, if I find you've disobeyed a direct order, I'll have you up on charges so fast your head will swim."

Without saying a word, Quick Killer went out, closing the door quietly behind him. It took all of his self-control not to slam it. Striding toward his horse, he pondered the setback. Gradually, a sly smile spread across his bronzed features. Yes, he would go after Chipota the Lipan, who raided the country to the north. But in order to deceive Chipota, who might have spies everywhere, he would have to take a roundabout trail getting there. The way he saw it, the wisest thing to do was to swing around to the southwest and circle until he reached Lipan country. And if, in so doing, he just happened to cut through the heart of the Chiricahua and Dragoon mountains, that was sheer coincidence.

Quick Killer didn't care what Captain Parmalee said. The threat of being disciplined held no weight with him. All that mattered was being the best. All that concerned him was his reputation. Delgadito—and the so-called White Apache—would be his, and no one else's.

Chapter Three

Had the warrior in the blue coat fired at the very second he sighted down his barrel at Delgadito, the lives of many innocents would have been spared. But the man hesitated to be sure of his shot, and in doing so he drastically altered the destiny of Arizona, for the worse.

For in those fleeting seconds of delay, Clay Taggart had time to leap to his feet and charge while venting an Apache war whoop and jamming his Winchester to his right shoulder. He snapped off a round, but the warrior in the blue coat spun at the same instant and the slug tore into the ground inches from the man's torso. Then Clay angled behind a tree to weather the return fire. But there was none. Peeking out, he was astonished to see the three warriors retreating north-ward as rapidly as their legs could carry them.

The undergrowth crackled and the four renegades appeared, rifles at the ready. Delgadito, Cuchillo

Negro, Fiero, and Ponce looked around for the source of the commotion they had heard. Clay immediately revealed himself, pointed at the fleeing men, and yelled in the Apache tongue, "They were going to shoot Delgadito."

With a yip the bloodthirsty Fiero was off in pursuit, bounding like a tawny cougar after panicked antelope, the jagged scar on his brow flushed scarlet from the excitement. Among a race that prided itself on its warlike qualities, he was the most warlike of all Chiricahuas. Fiero lived for the thrill of combat, for the pounding of his blood in his veins, for the fresh scent of the spilled blood of enemies in his nostrils. He was always at the forefront of every clash, spurred by his unbridled ferocity.

Second after the firebrand ran Ponce, the youngest member. Ponce, who had joined Delgadito to earn recognition and honor as a warrior, had of late begun to entertain doubts about the leader he had once thought the greatest of all. The slaughter of their fellows by scalp hunters had greatly shaken his confidence in Delgadito's ability, shaken it so badly that recently Ponce had toyed with the notion of abandoning the life of a renegade for life on the reservation. Despite his feelings, when his companions were threatened he was quick to spring to their defense.

Last to join the chase were Delgadito and Cuchillo Negro, the former the tallest of the four and next to Fiero the most superbly muscled. He presently pulled ahead of his companion and was in turn overtaken by the White Apache.

Clay Taggart looked at Delgadito, thinking that after so many days of being given the cold shoulder he had at last regained Delgadito's respect by saving the Apache's life. But the warrior didn't so much as glance around. And moments later a shot reminded him that he had to concentrate on the matter at hand if he intended to live long enough to smooth relations.

The fleeing trio had halted. Clay saw them seek cover behind pines and he dived for the ground as they commenced firing with a vengeance. The rest of the band did the same, Fiero the first one on their side to cut loose from behind a boulder.

Lead whizzed over Clay's head, clipping needles off the low branch of a tree. He fixed a bead on the stocky one who had taken his jerky but the man ducked back before he could squeeze the trigger. The exchange lasted less than a minute. Then the three ambushers broke and resumed their flight.

Once again Fiero led the pack of pursuers, whooping lustily and firing at random. Clay marveled at the hothead's audacity, for Fiero took risks more sensible men wouldn't take in a million years.

But Fiero didn't see it that way. He took calculated gambles, nothing more. He was a master at reading the intention of an adversary by the man's posture and reacting with his lightning swift reflexes before his life was put in serious jeopardy. Already he had observed that the warrior in the blue coat was the leader of the three strangers, and that whenever that warrior looked back and scowled, all three were certain to fire a volley seconds later. Now the warrior in blue did just that, and Fiero fell flat. Their bullets zinged harmlessly past.

Clay had crouched behind a log. He braced the Winchester barrel on top and once more tried to get the stocky brave in his sights. As before, the elusive threesome wheeled and sped off as he touched his finger to the trigger. Their shoot-and-run tactic was proving successful in that they had gained a wider lead. Afraid that they would escape, Clay poured on the speed.

There had been a time not long ago when Clay Taggart would have been left in the dust in a foot race with Apaches. But the months spent among them had steeled his sinews to a degree he never would have believed possible. Wilderness living had that effect on a man. Either he hardened, or he died. There was no place in the wild for the weak and the lazy.

Clay could jog for half a day without tiring. He could go two days without water, three without food. He had learned to ride for twenty-four hours at a stretch and not need sleep. He had become so much like an Apache that the other members of the band had regarded him as one of their own until Amarillo's death. And, oddly, he liked the change.

The fleeing warriors came to a glade and bore to the right. Both the stocky Apache and the man in the coat inadvertently pulled ahead of the third warrior when he paused to reload his rifle.

Snapping his Winchester up, Clay stroked the trigger a hair before Fiero and Delgadito. Their enemy staggered backward, clutched his chest, and toppled like a felled tree. Both the stocky one and blue coat stopped, but only momentarily. They plunged onward when they realized their friend was beyond help.

Apaches weren't prone to giving their lives needlessly for their fellows. Warriors who did so were branded fools and seldom spoken of highly unless they had been mortally wounded when they made the sacrifice. In such instances, since they already had nothing to lose, they would fight with a desperate fury, sometimes keeping an entire company of soldiers at bay while their people made good their escape.

The Apache attitude stemmed from the two main precepts of their existence: to steal without being caught, and to kill without being slain. To these ends the men were trained from infancy. Obtaining plunder and conducting warfare were all that interested them. And it went without saying that in order to enjoy plundering and killing, they had to be alive.

Fiero was the first to reach the fallen warrior. Hardly slowing, he nevertheless bashed the man's head with the stock of his rifle to ensure the warrior was dead.

Clay stayed abreast of Delgadito. He saw the Apache glance at their slain foe but observed no flicker of recognition. Meanwhile, the stocky warrior and blue coat had stopped pausing to fire every so often and were in full flight. The pair had changed direction, bearing to the northwest. Clay suspected they were making for their horses.

No one whooped or yipped, not even Fiero. The race was conducted in somber silence, with each man driving himself to his limit. The fleeing twosome no longer gained any ground, nor did Clay and his companions gain any. Through the woods to the north edge of the meadow the chase progressed, and it was here that luck favored the renegades.

Grazing nearby were a dozen horses. The man wearing the army coat went by without a second look, but the stocky warrior darted toward the animals. He lunged at a sorrel, caught hold of its mane, and went to swing up when the horse caught his strange scent and pranced skittishly to one side. Holding on, the stocky warrior ran awkwardly beside it, trying not to lose his footing. Abruptly, the horse spun, throwing the man off-balance. He stumbled and fell to his knees, his rifle flying from his hand. Frantically he reached for it, but it was beyond his grasp.

Fiero hurtled through the air and slammed into the stocky warrior, knocking the man flat. Quickly, the stocky Apache pushed to his knees, his knife flashing from its sheath. Fiero swung his Winchester, striking the gleaming blade and batting it aside. He then pivoted, ramming the muzzle into the other warrior's stomach. The stocky Apache doubled over but recovered almost immediately and flung himself to the left as Fiero went to strike him on the head.

Fiero intended to take the man alive. There were questions that had to be answered, and Fiero was a master at persuading captives to talk. He leveled his rifle and prepared to shoot, to wound, not to kill.

Suddenly a shot rang out to Fiero's rear. A hole blossomed in the center of the stocky warrior's broad chest. He looked down at the blood oozing forth, then snarled at Fiero. Fiero put a slug in the warrior's head.

Ponce ran up, beaming in triumph. "I shot him first," the younger man boasted.

Fiero had to resist an urge to lash out. "You did fine," he said sarcastically. "Now all we have to do is learn how to talk to dead men and we will know who sent him and why."

In a burst of insight Ponce understood the reason his companion was so upset. He felt like a chastened child for having fired, and he was about to explain that in the excitement of the chase he had simply gotten carried away when the White Apache and Delgadito passed them and Fiero dashed in their wake.

Quick Killer

Clay had gained the lead. He could see the warrior in the army coat dozens of feet ahead on the timbered slope, still running smoothly with no evidence of being fatigued. Whoever the man was, he knew how to pace himself and had the stamina of a mustang. Clay fell into a steady rhythm, avoiding obstacles and thickets where necessary. The warrior came to the bench and bolted past the lean-to.

Breaking into the open, Clay pumped his legs for all they were worth. Behind him pounded Fiero and the others, each eager to be the first to get his hands on their enemy. Clay was determined not to let them outstrip him. He would do it himself, thereby demonstrating once again that he was worthy of being one of their number.

The slope steadily steepened. Clay ran on the balls of his feet, digging them in for better traction. Several times he had clear shots but didn't avail himself of the opportunities. He'd seen Fiero's expression when Ponce shot the stocky warrior and knew they needed the last one alive.

The man fleeing for his life knew it too. He glanced over his shoulder repeatedly, and when he discovered that the White Apache was narrowing the gap, he pushed himself recklessly.

Clay had one thing in his favor. He knew the vicinity better, had trekked the length and breadth of the canyon. He knew the slope they were climbing eventually flattened out on a high ridge. It was there, he figured, the three warriors had tied their mounts.

The man in the army coat might have made it if not for another fluke of fate. A maze of thorny brush barred his ascent so he cut to the left. In so doing, he encountered a handful of downed saplings uprooted during a storm. Normally he would have negotiated them with ease, but today he was in such a hurry that he misjudged a step and his foot caught on one. He crashed down, throwing out his arms to catch himself.

Clay had the chance he needed. He took three more long steps and leaped, his Winchester angled on high for a stroke that would have knocked the warrior out had it landed. But the Apache was a credit to his tribe. He rose on one knee and whirled just as Clay pounced. Their bodies collided and together they tumbled down the slope.

They rolled over a dozen feet, until Clay's shoulder smashed into a tree trunk. At that juncture a knife magically materialized in the warrior's hand, and Clay used the Winchester to deflect a stab to the throat. Racked by pain, he pushed upright barely in time to keep the Apache from burying the knife in his chest. The warrior swung again, striking the barrel, and Clay's finger accidentally tightened on the trigger.

The Winchester blasted.

To Clay's dismay, he saw the slug catch the warrior high in the shoulder and lift the man off his feet. The Apache fell against a small ponderosa, his knife falling from nerveless fingers. Game to the last, the warrior got his other hand under him and began to rise.

Piercing whoops heralded the arrival of Fiero and Ponce. They bowled the other Apache over and Fiero wound up astride his chest. In seconds they had battered him near senseless and roughly jerked him erect.

Fiero looked at the bleeding wound, then at Clay. "You are as bad as Ponce, Lickoyee-shis-inday," he commented. "We needed one alive."

"I know, friend," Clay answered, using the word intentionally. While initially Fiero had hated him and despised having him in the band, at the time of Amarillo's death Fiero had come to accept the fact and been acting downright friendly on occasion. "My rifle went off by accident."

"There are no accidents. Only mistakes made by those who are too careless for their own good."

Clay was inclined to debate the point. But the nape of his neck abruptly prickled as if from a heat rash, and at the same time the two Apaches glanced up and over his head at someone behind him. Fearing there might have been a fourth ambusher no one had noticed, he spun to find Delgadito watching them.

"Take him to our camp, Fiero. We will get the answers we need there."

As always, Delgadito's features were the most inscrutable of all. Rarely could anyone read his thoughts. Clay Taggart would have given anything to know what was going through the former leader's mind. Yet had he known, he would have been shocked. For at that precise instant Delgadito, the Apache, was reflecting on how unfortunate it was that Taggart had survived the fight. In his cold heart Delgadito harbored an unquenchable thirst for revenge on the man who had spoiled his carefully laid plan to regain a role of trust and prestige in the Chiricahua tribe.

Once Delgadito had been a widely respected warrior. Once other warriors had flocked to join him on raids, had reveled in his victories and delighted in their share of the spoils taken. Once his name had been bandied about in the same breath as that of Mangus Colorado, Cochise, and Gokhlayeh. Then disaster had struck.

Delgadito had refused to bow to the white man's rule and fled into Mexico with a large number of followers. Scalp hunters drove them back across the border and later took them by surprise, slaughtering warriors, women, and children as if they were sheep. Only Delgadito and five others had survived.

For Delgadito, it would have been better had he died with the rest. He not only lost his wife, his relatives, and most of his friends, but he lost something he considered more precious. He lost his standing among the Chiricahuas. Where before he was regarded as a man of powerful medicine, now he was widely viewed as bad medicine, as someone the *Gans* had turned against and brought to ruin. No one wanted anything to do with him.

Delgadito had refused to give up hope. He had always prided himself on being adept at *na-tse-kes*, at the deep thinking that distinguished the common warrior from the great one. All Apaches of note were highly regarded for this virtue, and he had honed his skill to a degree seldom known.

He had schemed to have the white-eye he had jokingly named White Apache lead his small band on raids against those who had left Taggart for dead, dangling from a tree limb. He had hoped that a series of successful raids would go a long way toward changing the minds of his people. And he had intended, once White Apache outlived his usefulness, to reassume the leadership role rightfully his.

But everything that could go wrong had gone wrong. The *Nakai-hey* had captured Fiero, Ponce, and Amarillo, and it was White Apache who freed them. The scalp hunter responsible for the massacre of their band had given chase, and it was White Apache who tracked the butcher down and slew him.

Incredibly, Delgadito's few remaining followers turned to the white-eye for leadership, for the guidance they had formerly sought from Delgadito. White Apache's name became known among the Chiricahuas and other tribes, and everywhere it was mentioned in a more favorable light than Delgadito's.

Delgadito had seen the last wisps of power fading from his fingers as if they were tendrils of fading smoke. And the man he blamed, the man he wanted to destroy, was Clay Taggart. To that end, he was trying to poison the hearts of Fiero, Ponce, and Cuchillo Negro against the white-eye. To that end, he had blamed Amarillo's death on White Apache's bad medicine.

Now, as Taggart stood looking hopefully at him, Delgadito turned on his heel and followed Fiero and Ponce down the mountainside. Cuchillo Negro awaited them below and fell into step next to him.

"You did not run very fast," Delgadito said in tactful reproach.

"The last I knew, a *Shis-Inday* could run as fast as he pleased."

Delgadito cast a frown at the only man he regarded as a true friend. "Why must you twist my words all the time of late? Why has your heart grown so bitter toward me?"

"Lickoyee-shis-inday."

"What sorcery has he worked to turn you against me?"

"I am not against you so much as I am for him."

"You speak in riddles."

Cuchillo Negro pointed at the captive. "White Apache saved your life, yet still you seek to take his."

"Can you read another man's thoughts then?"

"Yours," Cuchillo Negro stated flatly. "I know you as I know myself. I know the trails your thoughts take, the secrets you share with no one else."

"Do you?" Delgadito tried to say with scorn that wasn't there. "One with so much power should be a medicine man, not a simple warrior."

"You hurl words as if they were rocks, yet you do not deny what I have said."

Delgadito slowed because he did not want anyone to overhear the next part of their conversation. Fiero and Ponce were yards off, hurrying onward. A look back showed White Apache sulking far behind. "I would speak straight tongue with you, my brother."

"My ears have always been open to Delgadito."

"Tell me why. The plain truth, nothing else."

Cuchillo Negro walked in silence for a bit, and seldom had Delgadito's nerves been so on edge. At last the former sighed. "The truth it will be, and it is truth born of our boyhoods together, of the many hunts we went on, the many grand times we had practicing the skills we would use when we became men. It is truth born of the manhood we have shared, of the many battles we have fought, the many hardships we have endured."

"What truth?" Delgadito said, scarcely able to conceal his impatience.

"The truth of your mistake."

"You promised you would speak with a straight tongue."

The warrior the Mexicans called Black Knife locked his gaze on Delgadito. "In all the winters we have known each other, I can count the mistakes you have made on one hand." He held up one finger. "And it is in this matter of the white-eye you took under your wing in order to soar among the clouds once again. You make a mistake in that you cannot see the good he can do not only for you but for all our people, the good only he could achieve because he is who he is. You make a mistake because you are thinking only of yourself. Think of the welfare of the entire tribe and you will see the wisdom of my words. I have walked with the bear. I know."

For once Delgadito was utterly confused. "You call that straight tongue? Of what possible good can this miserable white eye be to the Chiricahuas?"

"You have eyes but you do not see."

"See what?"

"That he can do for us what we have been unable to do for ourselves." Cuchillo Negro halted. "White Apache can free the Chiricahuas from the white man's yoke."

Chapter Four

The building was as brown and stark as the land on which it sat. A hovel, really, situated in the middle of a vast nowhere, with heaps of refuse piled out back and scruffy mongrels out front sniffing at the heels of everyone who entered.

And a lot of people did visit through the course of an average day, the majority Apaches from the reservation who broke the law to warm their bellies with the firewater to which they were addicted. The authorities knew about the hovel, and the man who ran it, but they made no attempt to put him out of business. In the army's opinion, drunken Indians were little threat, so the Apaches were permitted to inebriate themselves with unofficial sanction.

Much to the delight of Santiago Pasqual, the owner of the run-down saloon. Half Mexican, half Cibeque Apache, and all greed, he made his living selling watered down whiskey to the gullible reservation braves and hoarding the profits for his eventual move to Sonora where he planned to buy a large estate and live out his later years in comfort.

There was little actual work involved. Santiago poured drinks, wiped tables, and had his woman make *burritos, tacos,* or *enchiladas* for those of his customers who arrived hungry. It was fortunate for her she liked to cook because Santiago kept her at the stove twelve hours a day.

Occasionally there was trouble. Drunks were always cantankerous, and Santiago sometimes had to pull his scattergun out from under the bar and remind whoever was raising cane that buckshot meant burying. Usually the shotgun quieted them down. If not—well, he'd had to shoot a few over the years but there had never been a problem with the law. The ones he shot were always Apaches or breeds like himself.

On this day, Santiago leaned on the counter and idly observed the fourteen men scattered about the room. Three were playing cards in a dark corner. Two others were talking in low tones. Most simply sat staring with glazed eyes at the filthy walls, their precious bottles clutched in front of them.

Suddenly a shadow filled the doorway and Santiago glanced to his left, mildly surprised that someone had ridden up without him hearing. The figure was backlit by the sun, his face in dark shadow, and for a few moments Santiago was unable to distinguish more than a buckskin clad frame and a red headband. Then the man entered, a rifle held in the crook of an elbow, and all activity in the saloon ceased.

Santiago stiffened and gulped, his mouth going dry in the blink of an eye. Goose bumps broke out all over him as the newcomer walked to the bar and regarded him as he might a sidewinder about to strike. Santiago coughed to get his throat to work and said in greeting, "Tats-ah-das-ay-go. *Hola, amigo.*"

"I am not your friend," Quick Killer responded in flawless Spanish as he placed his .44-40 on the bar with a resounding thud that made several in the room jump.

"To what do I owe this honor?" Santiago asked, refusing to take insult since to do so would result in his death. "It has been six or seven months since you stopped by last."

Quick Killer surveyed the premises with disgust. "And nothing has changed, I see."

"Would you like a drink?" Santiago inquired to change the subject. He leaned on his elbows and spoke softly. "To show you I am not the bastard you seem to think, I will give you a bottle of my best. On the house."

"I did not come to this pigpen to slake my thirst," Quick Killer said indignantly. "I need information."

"And you think I can supply it? My humble self is flattered." Santiago gave his most ingratiating smile, a smile that always worked to pacify belligerent Americanos. It was his way of groveling without actually bending his knees, a way of showing he was as harmless as a fly. But this time it failed to impress. A hand of solid steel snaked out and pulled him halfway across the counter.

"Your humble self will not live out the day if you don't stop acting like the jackass you are and tell me what I need to know."

"Anything," Santiago said, embarrassed at being manhandled with all his customers looking on. "Please, Tats-as-das-ay-go. I did not mean to offend you."

Quick Killer let go and Pasqual slid back and

straightened. "Delgadito," the scout said.

"Again?" Santiago declared without thinking and hastily went on when the scout's hand moved toward him. "I can tell you no more than I did the last time!" He twisted, plucked a bottle of rye from a shelf, and poured himself a large glass. "Surely you heard about the raid? How Blue Cap wiped out nearly all of Delgadito's band? He has few friends left and no living relatives that I know of. So he never visits any of the villages. Never."

"What about those who ride with him?"

Santiago froze in the act of lifting the glass, then set it down so hard the rye splashed onto his hand. "They are hardly acquaintances of mine," he hedged.

"Still, you have heard things. You always hear things."

"Not this—," Santiago began, but stopped when the scout lifted a hand.

"Don't lie to me, dog. I know that Nah-kah-yen came to see you and that you gave him information about one of those who rides with Delgadito."

"Who told you such a thing?" Santiago responded, still stalling in the hope of scheming a way to turn the situation to his benefit. He didn't relish the prospect of having to give away something for nothing.

"None of your business," Quick Killer said. "Now tell me about Ponce and leave nothing out or I'll be back to visit you after I'm done in the mountains. And you wouldn't want that."

Santiago put his head closer to the other man's. "Have a heart, will you? Information is sometimes worth more than liquor. Nah-kah-yen paid me thirty dollars for the news I had learned. What will you give?"

"Something much more valuable than thirty dollars."

"Oh? What?"

"Your life."

One look into those snake-like eyes convinced Santiago that it was no empty threat. Sighing in frustration, he whispered, "All right. I will confide in you because I like you. But you must promise never to tell anyone where you obtained the information. Should Ponce hear, or anyone close to him, I would be in great danger."

"Do you really think I would tell a soul?"

"No," Santiago admitted. It was common knowledge that the only company Quick Killer kept was his own.

"Then start talking."

Santiago looked about to verify the drunks and card players were not paying any attention to him. "Several weeks ago a man came in. Old Coletto. Do you know him?"

"No."

"He stops by only now and then. Usually he hardly says a word, but this time I couldn't get him to shut his mouth." Santiago paused. "I think I gave him straight whiskey by mistake."

"Get to the point."

"While he was sobbing over the many sorrows in his life, he mentioned that his granddaughter was seeing a warrior who rode with Delgadito. He was quite proud of the fact. Claimed it was a man named Ponce, and went on and on about how Ponce was a credit to the Chiricahuas because he refused to give in to the white-eyes, and how if he was younger he'd be right out there with them and—"

"Where do I find this Coletto?"

"Palacio's village. He lives by himself. His wife died two winters ago and he hasn't been the same since."

56

Quick Killer

"Who else have you told this to?"

"Only Nah-kah-yen."

Quick Killer grunted and picked up his .44-40. "You will forget I was here. You will forget ever talking to me. You will forget Coletto paid you a visit. And you have never heard the name Ponce before. *Comprende?*"

"*Si. En este asunto me lavo las manos.*"

"You do well to wash your hands of it," Quick Killer said. Turning, he silently departed, with nary a ripple of the air to mark his passage.

Santiago Pasqual shivered as if it were icy cold and hastily gulped the rye down, savoring the burning sensation that warmed his throat and stomach. His larcenous nature prompted him to wonder how he might make a dollar or two off the scout's visit. There were a few people who would pay for the news, not the least of whom were Ponce's own family. But another shiver reminded him of the inevitable consequences should Quick Killer find out about his treachery. He filled the glass, then stared at the entrance. No, he decided, it would be smarter to check his impulse to make a dollar or two and let events play themselves out without his interference. He'd live longer that way. A lot longer.

Clay Taggart sat under his lean-to, staring into the crackling flames of the small fire he had started an hour ago, shortly after sundown. A glowing ember made a slight popping sound and reminded him of the noise made when Nah-kah-yen's fingers were broken one by one. Before his mind's eye flashed unbidden the long torture the scout had endured, the torture Clay had witnessed from grisly start to gory finish. He should have turned away, he reflected. Or, at the very least, he should have protested the barbaric acts the Apaches committed, yet he'd sat there and done nothing.

It was hard to say which upset Clay more. The torture, or the fact he hadn't felt the least bit upset about it. Never once had he felt queasy, never once had the atrocities bothered him. Not when the scout's lips were peeled from his face, not when Fiero chopped the man's toes off, not when Nah-kah-yen's abdomen was sliced open and his intestines pulled out. Yet, only a few months ago, Clay would have been sick to his stomach on seeing such savagery.

Clay leaned back and thoughtfully regarded the sparkling stars. What in the world was happening to him? he wondered. Had he gone plumb loco? Had living with the Apaches changed him that much in such a short time?

Nothing made sense anymore. Clay shook his head, recollecting a saying his grandpa had been fond of: Life was too ridiculous for words. And Clay had a feeling that it was going to get a lot worse before it got better.

The next second Clay had a different feeling, that of being watched. Without being obvious he placed his right hand on his rifle and drifted his gaze along the bench. He saw no one and chalked it up to a case of bad nerves until a shadow detached itself from the darkness.

Delgadito stepped into the flickering rosy light and halted. "May I join you, Lickoyee-shis-inday?" he asked.

Flabbergasted, Clay nevertheless collected his wits and beckoned. "You are welcome at my fire any time," he said. For the life of him he couldn't explain the warrior's visit, and he sat tense with expectation as the Apache hunkered down and switched to English.

"What you think of scout?"

"He got his due, I reckon," Clay said.

"You speak with straight tongue?"

"Yes," Clay answered, and repeated it louder, realizing he truly did believe justice had been served. "Those three varmints tried to bushwhack us. If I hadn't spotted them, all four of us would be pushing up flowers come spring. They got what was coming to them, sure enough."

Delgadito looked down at the ground. "You save my life, White Apache. I treat you bad and you save my life."

Clay wouldn't have been more shocked had Delgadito announced he'd repented of his misdeeds and wanted to turn himself over to the army. "Hell, partner. You haven't been treating me that badly."

"I have," Delgadito insisted. "There is much I must say to you to set things right."

"I'm listening," Clay said. In all the time he'd been with the renegades, he'd never heard a single warrior apologize for anything. For Delgadito to do so meant more to him than he cared to concede because he was more attached to the Apache than he cared to admit. He'd been flattering himself that the two of them were made from the same leather, and then Delgadito had up and yanked the rug out from under him. Maybe, he mused, the Apache had come to his senses.

Ironically, Delgadito was thinking the exact same thing, but his motives were far different than Clay suspected. His fruitful talk with Cuchillo Negro had persuaded him that he had indeed made a mistake, which he was about to rectify. So, folding his brawny hands in his lap, he began in his own tongue. "Do you understand good medicine and bad medicine, Lickoyee-shis-inday?"

"I believe I do," Clay said.

"When a warrior dies on a raid it is considered very bad medicine. We do not go near the place where he dies ever again." Delgadito picked up a stick and poked it in the fire. "Losing Amarillo was bad medicine. Because we lost him on a raid to wipe out your enemies, we blamed you for his death."

"I did all I could—" Clay started to object, but let it drop when the warrior resumed.

"We know you did not want him to die. We know you planned your raids carefully, as a *Shis-Inday* always should. But we blamed you anyway," Delgadito said. "To understand, you must see the world through our eyes. You must think like we think, believe as we believe."

"I am trying," Clay stated.

"You were born a white-eye. We should not blame you for that since none of us has control over such matters. But when you first came among us, we naturally saw you as an outsider. Your ways were not our ways and our ways were not yours."

Clay merely nodded. Apaches were reared to regard everyone not of their tribe as an enemy, and given the suffering they had endured at the hands of the Spaniards, Mexicans, and later his own kind, their outlook couldn't be faulted.

"Even after you had ridden with us on raids, we did not think of you as one of us. You were still the *Americano*. You were still not to be trusted." Delgadito tossed a stick into the flames. "Then you saved the others from the *Nakai-hey* and killed Blue Cap. You worked hard to learn our ways, to speak our tongue."

"Very hard," Clay threw in.

"And for a while we thought of you as one of us and all was well. But old habits die hard. When

Amarillo died, we again saw you as an outsider. We wanted nothing to do with you."

"And now?" Clay asked hopefully.

"Now I am here to say that our fire is your fire. We would like you to be one of us again. We want you to lead us on more raids."

"What?" Clay exclaimed, dazzled by his good fortune. With the Apaches once again under his thumb, he could continue his campaign of vengeance against the posse members who had strung him up and the man who had put them up to it, Miles Gillett. He was so elated that for a span of seconds he forgot about Cuchillo Negro's warning. On remembering, he eyed Delgadito suspiciously. "What is in this for you?"

The question surprised the warrior. Never before had the white-eye presumed to question his motives, which had secretly amazed and amused him. Apaches learned early on to never take anything for granted, to always look for the underlying reasons behind the actions of others. Delgadito believed that Lickoyee-shis-inday was too trusting for his own good. Perhaps, at last, he mused, the white-eye had learned not to trust anyone. "You know the thoughts of your kind better than we do. With you leading us, we will outsmart them at every turn. We will kill many whites and take much plunder."

"And what if another warrior dies?" Clay asked. "Do I take the blame again?"

"No. All that concerns us is the fight to rid ourselves of those who invaded our country and herded our people onto the reservation. Many sleeps ago we took an oath to resist with our lives, if need be, and that is what we will do."

"I see," Clay said.

But Delgadito had only detailed part of the reason. The warrior hadn't gone into his personal agenda, into the new long range plan he had to regain his leadership role. Nor did Delgadito see fit to mention the part Cuchillo Negro wanted Clay to play in reviving the flagging spirit of the entire Chiricahua tribe.

"I don't mind telling you, pard, that I'm right pleased at how things have turned out," Clay said good-naturedly in English. "I figured we'd never smoke the peace pipe and was set to light a shuck for parts unknown."

"Now we are friends again?"

"We sure are," Clay declared. "Now that we've mended fences, we can get on about the business of seeing that those vermin who made me the guest of honor at their necktie social pay for what they did." He saw the Apache smile and assumed it was with pleasure at having mended fences.

Actually, Delgadito was showing his derision at how easy it had been to manipulate Clay. During his short stay on the reservation, Delgadito had learned about the strange eagerness of the whites to readily forgive those who did them wrong. The trait ran contrary to all that Apaches believed, and he had been unable to comprehend how any people could pride themselves on exhibiting such weakness. But since they did, and since any and every weakness of an enemy was to be exploited, he had learned to take advantage of their stupidity.

"When do you want to go on the next raid?" Clay asked.

"When you are ready," Delgadito said.

"I'm ready now. We can head out at first light if it's all right with you." Clay chuckled in anticipation. "The next no-account on my list is a gent named

Jack Bitmer. We can be at his spread in three days. He has a sizeable herd of thoroughbreds, and some cattle besides if we want to go to all the trouble of driving them back to the reservation."

"We will see."

Clay touched a finger to his coffee pot. "The Arbuckle's about done. Care for a cup?"

Delgadito was more inclined to return to his fellow warriors, but his mouth seemed to have a will of its own. "I stay."

Rummaging in a pouch, Clay produced his battered tin cup and filled it. "Here. After you." He sat back as the warrior sipped loudly. "I've been doing a lot of thinking the past few days and I've got some notions worth sharing."

"My ears are open."

"Having lived with you a spell, I'm beginning to see that the Apaches and I have a lot in common."

"You think so?"

"Look at the facts," Clay said. "I had my ranch stolen out from under me by a greedy *hombre* who wants me dead. The Chiricahuas had their freedom stripped from them by a whole passel of greedy politicians who think the only good Apache is a dead one."

The similarity hadn't occurred to Delgadito and he remarked as much.

"There's more," Clay stated. "I'm now a wanted man because I had the gumption to fight for what is mine. You and the rest of your band are all wanted men because you had the grit to fight for what is yours."

"We are much the same," Delgadito conceded, the comparison sparking a new train of thought.

"I'm not done yet," Clay said. "I reckon I speak for both of us when I say that I'm not about to give up while a breath of life remains in my body."

"You do."

"So since we have so much in common, doesn't it make a heap of sense for us to work together to help one another get what we want?"

Delgadito took another swallow. He suspected where their conversation was leading and couldn't believe how smoothly things were working out. "We help you kill your enemies," he said.

"For which I'm grateful as can be," Clay said. "That's why I gave you a hand rubbing out Blue Cap. But you've helped me more than I've helped you, and I've always been a firm believer in paying my debts in full."

"Meaning?"

"Meaning there has to be more I can do on your behalf. I don't exactly know how, but I bet if you give it some thought you can come up with a few ideas."

"Maybe we can," Delgadito said, and it was all he could do not to yip in triumph. The white-eye had played right into their hands.

"I'm serious," Clay asserted. "I can be of big help to you. I spent a lot of time at the different forts when I delivered beef to the army. I know how they operate, and I think I can help you beat them at their own game." He watched a moth flit past. "Since I'm white, if I'm careful I could probably mingle among them without anyone being the wiser and learn all sorts of important information."

"You have this well thought out, Lickoyee-shis-inday."

"You're damn right I do. Since the law and the army have seen fit to brand me an outlaw and a renegade, I guess I might as well live up to the lies they're spreading about me. The Taggart clan has never backed down from a scrape yet and I'm not about to break the family tradition." Clay stared somberly into the night. "The White Apache, I'm called. Well, that suits me just fine. From here on out I'm going to be the wildest, fiercest, meanest, damned Apache anyone has ever seen. By the time I'm done, they'll tremble in their boots at the mention of my name."

Chapter Five

The village of Palacio had quieted for the night when Quick Killer made his move. From before sunset until close to midnight he crouched in the chaparral and observed all that transpired. He saw children playing, women working on skins and cooking and gossiping. He watched warriors gamble, clean their rifles, sharpen their knives. No one had the slightest idea he was there, not the deer hunters he had crept past high in the rocks, not the dogs that were unable to detect his scent because he had smeared himself with horse dung, and certainly not the reservation warriors who had lost their razor edge from too much soft living.

Quick Killer had nothing but contempt for reservation Indians. They were pale imitations of the men they had once been, the course of their lives set by their white masters. He held the renegades he tracked down in higher regard than he did these pathetic prisoners of their own cowardice.

When the last of the men had entered their wicki-ups, Quick Killer edged closer to the village. There were dozens of dwellings but only one housing an old man who lived by himself. Quick Killer had made doubly certain, memorizing all the comings and goings of everyone.

The old man had picked well. His wickiup was situated at the base of a knoll in a secluded spot that afforded shade in the day and protection from the wind at night. The interior was dark.

Quick Killer glided like a panther to the end of the brush, then moved swiftly to the wall of the conical structure. Circling around to the front, he pointed his rifle at the entrance and said softly in Apache, "Coletto, come out."

There was a rustling noise and the wizened features of the aged warrior appeared. "Who calls me?"

"Tats-ah-das-ay-go."

The old man recoiled, then seemed to see the Winchester for the first time. "What does Quick Killer want with me?"

"Ponce."

"I know no one by that name."

Quick Killer slid closer so that the rifle muzzle almost touched Coletto's wide nose. "Allow me to refresh your memory. He is the young man who pays your granddaughter visits. The same young man who rides with Delgadito."

"And it is Delgadito you really want." Coletto frowned. "I have heard many stories about you, scout. They say a man must have a death wish to cross you. But I tell you now that I will not say anything."

"You care for this Ponce that much?"

"I hardly know him. It is Delgadito I think of. He is the last true *Shis-Inday*."

The disclosure unsettled Quick Killer. He had intended to barter Ponce's life for the information he needed. "So you will not tell me in which lodge I can find your granddaughter?"

"Never."

"You are wrong, old one," Quick Killer said, and slammed the .44-40 against the venerable warrior's head twice in such swift succession the rifle was a blur. Coletto fell from sight. Quick Killer took a moment to scan the village and verify no one had seen, then he drew his long hunting knife and slipped within.

For the next two hours little stirred in the village of Palacio. Once a mongrel strayed by Coletto's wickiup and lifted its head on smelling the tangy scent of blood. It padded to the opening, sniffing loudly, and it was still sniffing when an iron hand flashed out and grabbed it by the scruff of the throat while at the same instant a dripping knife was plunged between its ribs three times. The animal went limp and was dragged inside.

Presently Quick Killer reappeared. He stared at a particular dwelling a while, turned, and melted into the chaparral. A circuitous route brought him to the trail the women took every morning on their way to the spring for water. He hiked to the pool, a distance of forty yards, and drank his full. A convenient thicket provided the cover he needed, and he sat down in the middle of it to wait. A few hours before dawn he lowered his chin to his chest and slept, awakening when the first pale streaks of pink framed the eastern horizon.

Soon the early risers came, mostly married women who had husbands and children to feed. The younger, single women came later, usually in pairs or threes, chattering gaily. Quick Killer studied them, seeking one wearing a red shawl, and half an hour after sunrise she came, with one other. He listened closely and heard her name. Ko-do. It meant Firefly.

The two women knelt to fill their clay water jars. Another woman was just leaving. Quick Killer didn't move until she was gone around a bend, then he rose, slipped from the brush, and was behind the two young ones before either suspected. The friend of Ko-do's started to look up. Quick Killer buried his knife between her shoulder blades, then smashed the hilt against Ko-do's chin as she whirled.

Swiftly Quick Killer dropped to his right knee, slid the knife into its beaded sheath, and slung the unconscious maiden over his shoulder as if she were a sack of grain. He checked the trail as he picked up his rifle. No one else had shown yet but it was only a matter of minutes.

Quick Killer hastened into the brush, making for the high ground where he had left his calico. For hundreds of feet he walked on solid rock. Once at the horse, he laid Ko-do over its back and mounted. From the vicinity of the spring issued a screech attended by loud shouts, and he knew that within a short while there would be Chiricahuas scouring every square inch of undergrowth for a mile around.

Lifting the reins, Quick Killer jabbed his heels and galloped down into a ravine that brought him to a lowland plain covered with mesquite. He rode on until the sun was straight overhead. In a narrow gorge he drew rein and roughly dumped the woman on the ground. She stirred, moaning faintly.

Dismounting, Quick Killer ground-hitched the calico and squatted beside Ko-do. He admired her rosy lips, noted the fullness promised by the fit of her clothes. And he reflected that rarely had a manhunt brought him so much pleasure.

Many miles away another man was equally pleased by a turn of events. Clay Taggart rode beside Delgadito at the head of the renegade band, heading westward toward the San Pedro River. He was glad to have been accepted by the Apaches again, and gladder still that he could continue his vendetta against those who had wronged him.

So far Clay had accounted for two of the twelve posse members. That left ten men who were going to die, eleven counting Miles Gillett, the cagey master-mind who had framed him for murder and stolen the woman he had once loved.

Clay planned to save Gillett for last. He wanted the bastard to know what was coming, to experience the same gnawing helplessness that Clay had felt as the noose was tightened around his neck. For as long as Clay lived he would never forget that awful ordeal, in particular that terrible moment when his fiery lungs had been fit to burst and his vision had dimmed to black as he balanced on the brink of oblivion. It was the spur that pricked his conscience every time he dared think about turning back from the vengeance trail. It was his single greatest motivation in life.

The chestnut gave a snort and pricked its ears. Clay immediately scoured the landscape but saw no cause for alarm. He complimented himself on being able to convince the Apaches into using horses instead of going afoot as they were accustomed to doing when on raids. Granted, on foot they could exercise greater stealth and would leave fewer tracks. But what they lost in that regard they made up for in being able to go faster and covering more ground at a single stretch. Plus, they could make meals of their mounts should game prove scarce.

Suddenly, Clay's chestnut nickered lightly. Clay saw Delgadito give it a sharp glance, reminding him that Apaches wouldn't abide a noisy horse. Any animal that loved to hear itself neigh invariably wound up simmering in a stew pot. He leaned forward to throttle the chestnut so it wouldn't whinny again when his nose registered the faint odor of wood smoke.

All the Apaches drew rein at the selfsame moment Clay did. The sluggish wind blew toward them from the northwest, across the arid plain they were crossing. Except for scattered islands of scrub trees and waving strands of dry grass, there was scant cover, certainly not enough to hide a camp or a fire. He looked at the warriors and found them looking at him. "Cuchillo Negro," he said.

The lean warrior swung down, handed the reins to Ponce, and sped off across the plain. In seconds he had blended into the land, becoming invisible.

Clay never tired of marveling at the uncanny ability of his companions. No matter how hard he tried, he couldn't duplicate all their feats although he came close in more regards than most. To kill the time, he turned to Delgadito and whispered in Apache, "It is good to be on the war path again."

The warrior grunted. "You are more *Shis-Inday* than you think," he said softly. "Maybe your mother stole you from an Apache woman when you were a baby."

That was the first and only joke Clay had ever heard Delgadito make, and he was so taken aback he nearly blundered and laughed aloud. Instead, he caught himself and whispered in English, "The longer I ride with you, the more I like it. I don't mind confessing it's got me a mite worried."

"Why worry?" Delgadito responded. "You like Apaches, you stay with Apaches. Always welcome."

"I'm obliged, pard," Clay said, and meant it, but at the same time he was mystified by the warrior's complete change in attitude. One day Delgadito wouldn't have anything to do with him, the next Delgadito acted as if they were best friends. There was no explaining the *Shis-Inday* sometimes.

The next five minutes were spent in alert silence. Finally Cuchillo Negro popped up beside a hedgehog cactus. He jogged to the group and reported. "There are three hairy white-eyes camped in a gully. They have extra horses, and many packs of furs."

"Poachers," Clay deduced. Ever since the U.S. government signed a treaty with the Chiricahuas, the area embracing the Dragoon and Chiricahua Mountains was exclusively theirs. No whites were to hunt or trap anywhere within the reservation boundaries. But the treaty hadn't stopped poachers from helping themselves to the land's bounty whenever they were of a mind. To Delgadito, he said in English, "They must be on their way to Tucson to sell their hides. They probably only travel at night to avoid army patrols, and right now they're lying low until dark. What do you reckon we should do?"

Delgadito acted surprised. "We all agreed that you should lead us. So lead, Lickoyee-shis-inday."

Clay was inclined to suggest they should ride on and avoid the trappers until it occurred to him that here was a chance to show the warriors he meant what he had said about siding with them in their war on those determined to destroy their kind. The poachers had no business killing animals the Apaches needed to feed and clothe themselves. Maybe, he mused, he should make an object lesson of this bunch so others would think twice before trespassing on Apache territory. He faced the others. "We will kill these whites and take everything they own."

The reactions of the four warriors differed. Delgadito was immensely pleased. Cuchillo Negro was too, but it also bothered him a trifle that White Apache was so readily falling into the pattern they wanted. Ponce hefted his rifle, eager to hone his fighting skills. And Fiero gazed on White Apache as if setting eyes for the first time on a kindred spirit.

"Leave your horses here," Clay ordered. "When we are in position, wait for my signal. Use your knives, not your guns. This must be quiet work."

The gully cut the plain from north to south. Twenty yards wide, it afforded the perfect spot to hide. Had the trappers not become hungry and started a fire to roast their meal, they would have been safe.

From the west rim Clay peered down at the three burly specimens and their haul. One was busy skinning a rabbit, the other two were puffing on pipes and talking. Piled against the east wall were twelves bound bales of beaver, cougar, and fox plews.

"—wait to get my share," a pipe smoker was saying in a low voice. "I'm fixin' to head for New Orleans and have me a grand time."

"Why go so blamed far?" asked the other. "What does New Orleans have that Denver and St. Louis don't?"

"Women. Droves of easy women sashaying their wares right there in the street."

"Hell, Denver and St. Louis have more fallen doves than you can shake a stick at. And they're a far sight closer."

"Don't care, Eb. I'm partial to New Orleans. Spent a lot of time there when I was sprout. You ain't lived until you've taken in the sights that wicked city has to offer."

"I'll take your word for it," Eb said. "Me, I'm heading for St. Louie, as I like to call it. Got me an old gal there who can wrap her legs around a man and not let go for a month of Sundays."

"Sure she'll recollect you after all this while?"

"Hell, yes," Eb said. "She don't get many gentleman callers as handsome as me."

"But I bet the others smell better."

The poachers chuckled.

On the rim, Clay hesitated to give the signal. It had been easy to pronounce judgment on the trappers when he hadn't set eyes on them. But now there they were: living, breathing human beings—white men like himself, men who must have kin somewhere, relatives who would mourn their loss. How could he rub them out with a gesture? Then he thought of his promise to the Apaches, and how much taking his revenge on Miles Gillett meant to him. His mouth a somber slit, he waved his rifle once.

The poachers never had a prayer. The four Apaches swooped into the gully like ferocious birds of prey, pouncing on the startled trappers before they could bring a rifle or pistol into play. Ponce and Cuchillo Negro closed on Eb, who clawed at a Colt as two knives ripped into his flesh. Fiero took the other poacher, his blade slicing to the hilt in the man's throat as the trapper foolishly tried to grab his arm.

74

Delgadito jumped on the man working on the rabbit. Since the poacher already had a knife in hand, he was able to leap erect and defend himself. He parried Delgadito's first few thrusts while frantically back-pedaling. Unfortunately for him, he neglected to keep an eye on the ground and didn't notice a saddle until his foot caught in it and he went down. Delgadito was on him in a twinkling, his knife sinking deep, not once but four times.

And just like that it was over. The three trappers lay in spreading puddles of blood, one motionless in death, another twitching convulsively, and Eb wheezing raggedly as tiny red geysers pumped from his chest.

Clay rose and walked to the bottom. He stood over Eb, saw the trapper's eyes widen.

"Your eyes! They're blue!" Eb erupted in a coughing fit, and when it subsided, said, "You're the one we heard about, aren't you? The White Apache?"

"I am," Clay admitted.

"How can you do this to white folk?" Eb asked. "How—" Whatever else he was going to say was lost to posterity when the poacher went limp, expiring his last in a long, loud breath.

The Apaches had already started stripping weapons from the dead, and Ponce was busy collecting the horses. Oblivious to them, Clay Taggart stared at Eb, trying to come to terms with the question the trapper had posed. On an impulse he leaned down and snatched Eb's hat, an old brown woolsey of the sort worn by prospectors, with the front brim folded up at a rakish angle and one side sloped from the crown to the brim. Clay couldn't say what prompted him to put the hat on.

Delgadito had seen and came over. "What you want with that?" he asked in English.

"I don't rightly know," Clay admitted.

"Hats for white-eyes, not a *Shis-Inday*."

"But I'm the *White* Apache, remember?" Clay said, and to avoid debating the matter further he pointed at the plunder and asked, "What do you suggest we do with all this stuff? We could cache the spoils but we can't very well leave the horses here until we come back this way next."

"One of us must take plunder to Sweet Grass."

"Who?"

"You are leader," Delgadito reminded him yet again.

Clay debated whom to pick. It couldn't be Delgadito since he didn't feel confident enough to handle the others without Delgadito's support. Cuchillo Negro was reliable so far as he knew, but he'd rather have Black Knife with him. Fiero was too hotheaded to be let loose on his own; there was no telling what the firebrand might do. All of which made his decision a simple one. "Ponce," he said in Apache, "will you take the trappers' belongings and animals to Sweet Grass and watch over them until we return?" He half expected an argument since Ponce was so keen on earning merit in warfare. To his surprise, the young warrior did not appear the least bothered. In fact, based on Ponce's expression, Clay suspected he was strangely pleased by the request.

"I will be glad to do so, White Apache."

Fiero was admiring a Colt he had taken from the poacher he slew. "You will miss out on all the fighting," he mentioned.

"There will always be more," Ponce said, and occupied himself gathering the possessions lying about.

Gratified that his decision had not been challenged, Clay climbed from the gully and headed toward the horses. He didn't look back to see if the rest followed. He just naturally took it for granted they would.

Delgadito was the first to catch up. "You do well, White Apache" he remarked in English.

"I reckon I'm getting the hang of being the cock-a-doodle do."

"The what?"

"The big sugar. The one who reads the Scriptures. The leader."

"Some yes, some no."

"I don't savvy."

"You ask Ponce to take plunder back."

"So? Should I have asked someone else?"

"Not that. *Shis-Inday* leader not ask. *Shis-Inday* leader tell."

"I thought Apaches were too independent to take orders. I didn't want to start barking commands at Fiero or someone else and have them turn on me."

"Most time *Shis-Inday* not take orders. In war we do. Always have war chief."

"Am I to take it that I'm the war chief of this outfit?"

"No. You White Apache. You special."

"Thanks, I think."

Once they were mounted, Clay bore to the northwest. They rode hard until an hour before sunset, at which time he led the Apaches in among manzanita to rest their animals. He had brought a pouch filled with jerky and shared it with the others. The warriors squatted on their haunches. He sat with his back to the cherry-red bark of one of the short trees and pushed his new hat back on his head. "I can't wait to see the look on Jack Bitmer's face when I bury my knife in his belly," he told Delgadito.

"How many others be ranchers?" the warrior asked.

"Denton and Socher. The rest of the men I'm after are gunnies, cowhands, and drifters."

"And marshal."

Clay hadn't forgotten about Tucson's top lawdog. Marshal Tom Crane was his name, and he was a cat's-paw controlled by Miles Gillett. Clay would never forgive Crane for the unsavory part the lawman had played in the lynching. In his estimation, when lawmen went around breaking the law there was no law, and it was time for ordinary folks to take matters into their own hands. Just like he was going to do.

Until late that night the band pressed on. Clay was so anxious to reach Bitmer's spread that he would have gone on until dawn, but common sense warned him not to. He slept lightly, as he always did on the trail, yet in spite of that he was up well before first light, feeling refreshed and raring to go. It was another example of the drastic change that had come over him since he'd been living as an Apache. During his ranching days he'd slept out many a night and always awoke the next morning suffering stiff muscles and tight joints.

Because Bitmer's ranch lay well to the north of Tucson, Clay bore in that direction. Toward the middle of the morning he guessed they were close to the road that connected Tucson to Mesilla far to the east, and he slowed the chestnut to a walk. Cavalry patrols traveled the road regularly to safeguard the steady stream of pilgrims using it, so he had to be careful not to blunder into one. Sometimes, as he'd learned the hard way, those patrols included Apache scouts who were every bit the equal of their renegade counterparts.

Clay was winding among dense brush when the rattle of wagon wheels carried to his ears through the hot, dry air. Reining up, he tied his animal and announced quietly, "I will go check. When you hear me whistle, bring my horse."

Keeping low, Clay advanced until he saw the dusty roadway ahead. A large saguaro stood close by it, and he quickly crawled into its shadow for a clear view in both directions. He thought he would see a farmer or rancher or perhaps a trader but instead spied two figures in a buckboard. And that wasn't all.

Escorting the buckboard was a full detachment of United States Cavalry.

Chapter Six

The Chiricahua maiden named Ko-do came awake with a start. She automatically sat up and fearfully glanced around, not knowing what to expect. The last thing she remembered was seeing her dearest friend collapse with blood spurting from a back wound, and then something had smashed her on the jaw. Now, she set eyes on a dark stranger in buckskins who was in the act of removing the short moccasins he wore in order to replace them with a different pair lying on the ground beside him.

"At last," the stranger said in her tongue. "Have a nice rest?"

Ko-do went to stand and discovered to her dismay that her ankles were bound. She reached for the rope but a low hiss from the stranger froze her midway.

"I would not do that, sweet Ko-do, unless you cannot wait to die."

Struggling to control the panic that threatened to overwhelm her, Ko-do swept their surroundings. They were in a rocky gorge close to a small spring. High overhead a lone buzzard circled as if waiting for a meal. A lump formed in her throat and she had to swallow before she could speak. "Who are you? What do you want with me?"

"I am called Quick Killer," the man said with exaggerated pride. "Perhaps you have heard of me?"

"No," Ko-do said.

The man grinned. "Then my reputation is not as widespread as I flattered myself to believe." He removed the second of the two short moccasins. "I am a scout, pretty one. A very special scout. The white-eyes pay me to track down renegades and ask no questions if I bring the renegades back slung over a horse. At the moment I am after Delgadito and the *Americano* known as the White Apache."

"What does this have to do with me?" Ko-do bluffed, knowing full well the answer.

"Please, woman. Do not insult me or I will make your end so painful you will plead with me to end your misery." Quick Killer lifted one of the knee-high moccasins at his side and began squirming a foot into it.

"Do the whites pay you to kill women?" Ko-do snapped, her fertile mind racing as she tried to scheme a way out of her predicament.

"No," Quick Killer said. "But what they do not know cannot hurt me." He commenced lacing up the moccasin.

"My people will know. They will report what you have done to the reservation agent and soldiers will come after you."

Quick Killer fixed her with a sneer. "How silly you are. Do you think I would be so careless?" He patted the short moccasins he had just removed. "These are Comanche. They belonged to a warrior I killed several winters ago. I wore them when I took you so that the men of your village will think a Comanche was to blame." He resumed lacing. "Your tribe and their tribe have been at war forever. It is nothing new for a warrior from one to steal a woman from another." Quick Killer grinned again and touched the knee-high moccasin he had just put on. "These are Chiricahua-made. I bought them from a Chiricahua scout at Fort Bowie before coming to the reservation. If any men from your tribe see my tracks now, they will think I am one of their own."

Ko-do saw her abductor in a whole new horrific light. She wriggled her legs to test her bonds and realized she could not possibly escape with him right there.

"The secret to staying alive in a world filled with enemies is to always be one step ahead of them," Quick Killer lectured her. "I have lived as long as I have only because I am never caught unprepared."

"My father and grandfather will find you. Nothing will keep them from tracking you down."

"Again you talk like a child and not a mature woman," Quick Killer said while putting on the other knee-high. "I took great pains to hide my trail. Your father will lead a search party but he will never find us." The scout paused. "As for Coletto, he has gone to meet his ancestors."

The shock drained the blood from Ko-do's fair face. "You killed my grandfather?" she asked, aghast.

"I needed to know your name and what you looked like. Old Coletto did not want to tell me, but after I had skinned him down to his waist he changed his mind."

Quick Killer

"You are worse than the Comanches!" Ko-do said, her grief dominating her. Without thinking, she added, "It's true what they say! Breeds like you are no better than animals! You live to torture and kill!"

The words were scarcely out of the maiden's mouth when Quick Killer was on her. He hit her twice, knocking her flat, her lips mashed and bleeding. "For that, bitch," he growled, "you will suffer far worse than the old one did."

"I do not care!" Ko-do blustered. "I will never tell you what you want to know!"

Quick Killer composed himself and sat on a nearby boulder. "Is Ponce that important to you? Do you love him so much you would endure pain such as you have never known in a stupid attempt to save him?"

"Ponce is going to take me for his wife soon. He has grown tired of the war path."

"Is that the lie he told just so he could fondle you?" Quick Killer said in contempt. "How could you believe him? Ponce is an Apache and Apaches live for war. I know, because my father was a White Mountain Apache."

Ko-do found the strength to prop herself on an elbow. "You waste your words, breed. I will not fall for your trick. Nothing you can say will convince me that Ponce does not love me." She gingerly touched her lower lip and felt the pulped flesh. "As for Ponce being Apache, almost all Apache men have given up the war path for reservation life. He will be doing no differently than they do."

"Then he is less of a man than I thought," Quick Killer said. He gazed almost wistfully at the distant horizon. "You might find this hard to accept, girl, but I admire men like Delgadito, men willing to fight for their freedom. Men who live according to the old ways. Men who will never give in to the *Americanos*."

"Yet you hunt them for the *Americanos!*"

Quick Killer regarded her sadly. "If I did not hunt them, I would be one of them. Do you understand?"

Ko-do was thoroughly confused. She was terribly scared and hurting but she refused to give her tormenter the satisfaction of seeing her cry or show weakness in any other respect. "All I understand is that you are a mad dog who kills his brothers in the name of those who are our enemies. Or maybe you are a coward at heart, too afraid to fight the whites yourself so you kill those who are braver than you."

The scout's gaze hardened. "Stupidity runs in your family, I see." He sighed. "Very well. Enough talk. Tell me where Delgadito's band is hiding out."

"Ponce has never told me," Ko-do declared, her heart fluttering in her chest like that of a panicked bird.

"You are a poor liar. Young lovers never keep secrets from one another."

"Delgadito made Ponce pledge never to reveal the locations of their camps."

Quick Killer rose. "I tire of this game, woman. I want the information and I want it now." He rested his hand on the hilt of his knife. "The choice is yours. Fast or slow. Which will it be?"

Ko-do was no fool. Until the white-eyes forced her people to adopt to reservation life, she had lived under the constant threat of attack by their many enemies. She had witnessed a raid by Navahos in which many Apaches had been slain; she had seen wounded warriors brought back to die. Violence and death had been a daily part of Apache life. So she knew the full consequences of her act when she squared her slender shoulders and announced, "Do with me what you will. I will not betray Ponce."

"We will see," Quick Killer said harshly as he slowly drew the knife and leaned over her. "Yes, we will most certainly see."

At the very moment that the woman who loved Ponce with all her heart saw a gleaming blade dip toward her body, the young warrior was on his way to Sweet Grass, a string of stolen horses laden with plunder strung out behind him.

Ponce was quite happy at the turn of events. He hadn't said anything to the others yet, but he had been pondering the merits of quitting the band and settling down ever since meeting a certain *ninya* in Palacio's village. At one time he would have banished such a thought from his head the instant it blossomed. He would have told himself women were unimportant in the Apache scheme of things. Ko-do though, was different. Try as he might he was unable to get her out of his mind.

Ponce knew that all men went through a similar period in their lives. From his father and his father's father he had learned that one day he would look on a woman and see her differently than he ever had any other female. As a boy and young man he had secretly scoffed when they mentioned it. His sole interest was in becoming the best warrior he could be, a man worthy of respect, perhaps a tribal leader one day.

So Ponce had been all the more surprised after he was introduced to Ko-do and could not stop thinking about her. She had become an obsession, and he knew he wouldn't be satisfied until she shared his wickiup.

Apache custom in affairs of the heart was clear-cut. A man interested in taking a woman to wife must tie his horse outside her father's lodge. If the woman left the animal standing there neglected for four days, it meant she wasn't interested. If, however, she fed the horse, took it to water, and tied it in front of her suitor's wickiup, it meant she had accepted.

Ponce intended to try his luck the next time he visited Palacio's village. He already knew Ko-do cared for him but he couldn't keep a tight knot of tension from forming in his gut every time he thought about putting her to the test. More than one warrior who believed he had a woman's heart in the palm of his hand was later shamed and made an object of ridicule when his poor horse was left to suffer thirst and hunger. Ponce didn't want that to befall him.

So preoccupied was the young warrior that he failed to note the slight swirl of dust to the southwest until it had grown in size to resemble a pale tornado. When he did spot it, he slowed, his brow knit in consternation.

A large body of horsemen were heading his way.

Only for a few seconds did Ponce stare at the cloud. Reining sharply to the left, he made for thick brush, tugging furiously on the lead rope to goad the string of horses into faster motion. He glanced over his shoulder at the wisps of dust his animals were raising and hoped the oncoming party wouldn't notice.

Ponce had no idea who the riders were but of one fact he could be sure; they wouldn't be friendly. Chiricahuas were restricted to the reservation so it was unlikely they were warriors from his own tribe. He suspected it was an army patrol. And if the soldiers spotted him, he wouldn't live out the day.

Quick Killer

Once in the brush, Ponce tied the lead rope to a limb, swung down, and dashed to the edge of the vegetation. He flattened behind a bush, his keen eyes roving the choking cloud until figures materialized, Indians in breechcloths and painted for war. They were Navahos, bitter enemies of the Chiricahuas.

Ponce counted eleven in all. They were riding westward, herding several dozen head of horses between them. Warriors returning from a raid, Ponce deduced. He stayed perfectly still, watching the main body go by. A few warriors rode behind the herd to urge the animals on. And fifty yards back rode a solitary brave whose job it was to keep an eye on their back trail. This man was the only one who had not yet passed by when one of the horses Ponce had secreted let out with a loud neigh.

The Navaho drew rein and glanced at the brush, then at the herd. The man started toward Ponce, but stopped, evidently uncertain whether the whinny had issued from the brush or the herd. He might have gone on had the horse in the brush not decided to let out with another cry. The Navaho worked the lever on his rifle and slowly advanced.

Ponce glanced at the retreating war party. So far none of the other warriors had noticed their companion was missing. Crawling backwards, he moved deeper into the growth and concealed himself in a stand of high brown grass.

The Navaho reached the brush and soundlessly slid to the ground. Holding the rifle at his waist, he padded toward the hidden horses, his lively eyes darting to and fro. He was in his middle years, an experienced warrior who would not be easily subdued.

Ponce let go of his rifle and drew his knife. He would rather use the gun but a shot would bring the

87

rest. The Navaho had crouched and was working from shrub to shrub. Ponce saw that the man would miss his hiding place and go by about ten feet to the left. He twisted, placing the knife close to his chest, his legs coiling under him.

Suddenly the Navaho halted and made a three hundred and sixty degree turn. He suspected something but saw nothing. More slowly than ever, he went on.

Ponce was coiled to spring. He didn't like having to cover so much distance but it couldn't be helped. The Navaho spied the stolen horses and crouched low to study them.

Rising, Ponce hurtled at the Navaho's back. He knew the warrior would hear him, knew the man would whirl, but he counted on his speed to get him there before the Navaho fired and his speed was equal to the occasion. He slammed into the warrior like a human battering ram. They both went down, the Navaho losing the rifle, Ponce almost losing his knife.

Ponce slashed, tearing into his enemy's leg but not deeply. Swift as a cat, the Navaho rose to his knees and whipped out his own blade. Ponce had to throw himself to the right as the warrior stabbed at his throat. He cut low, into the Navaho's other leg, which didn't stop the Navaho from lancing a blow at his shoulder. He felt the steel bite, felt blood seep out.

A push and a hop brought Ponce erect. The Navaho was just as quick and the two of them circled, seeking an opening. Ponce lunged high; the Navaho countered low. Neither scored but it was close both times.

In the back of Ponce's mind was the nagging thought that the other Navahos might soon miss

Quick Killer

the one he fought and ride back to investigate. He
had to dispatch his adversary swiftly but the Navaho
was a formidable fighter, wary and skilled.

As if to prove Ponce right, the Navaho feinted,
spearing his blade at Ponce's groin. Ponce automatically blocked the blade with his own. The Navaho
was expecting that and simply reversed direction,
swinging at Ponce's chest. By mere chance the knife
slipped between the young Apache's torso and his
arm, nicking his ribs.

Ponce retreated to give himself more room. He
noticed a smug smile on the Navaho but didn't
let it anger him. At an early age Chiricahua boys
were taught that the key to winning in battle was to
keep a clear head. Anger clouded judgment, dulled
reflexes.

The Navaho abruptly glanced westward and
opened his mouth to yell, an unexpected tactic, all
the more so because it would never have occurred
to Ponce to do the same. Apaches were staunch
believers in fighting their own battles. Even when
unevenly matched, rarely would a Chiricahua call
for aid.

But being caught off guard didn't stop Ponce from
acting. As the first sound started to issue from the
Navaho's mouth, Ponce launched a savage attack,
swinging in wide, controlled strokes that forced the
Navaho to devote his whole attention to staying alive,
the shout momentarily dying in his throat.

Ponce deliberately pressed the Navaho as hard as
he could. The warrior retreated under the onslaught,
their knives ringing together as they thrust and
blocked with ferocious intensity. Had their ages
been more equal, had the Navaho been as young as
Ponce, the outcome would have been decided in the
first few moments with Ponce the victor. Navahos

were formidable fighters in their own right, but man for man they were no match for the scourges of the Southwest.

This certain Navaho lost his smug smile and fought with renewed tenacity. He tried a flurry of cuts that would have slain most antagonists. His inability to deliver a fatal blow made him reckless, made him careless, so that when he came to the rim of a shallow basin he failed to notice it until his left heel slipped out from under him and he toppled backwards.

Ponce took a single step and leaped, his knife raised high as he came down on top of the scrambling Navaho. The warrior twisted and tried to spear Ponce in the belly but Ponce hit him before he could. Together they went down, Ponce sinking his blade in the other's shoulder.

The Navaho scrambled backward. Ponce went after him and sliced open the man's shin. Bending at the waist, the Navaho attempted to cleave Ponce's head from his shoulders but Ponce ducked underneath the Navaho's flashing arm and drove his knife into the man's armpit. Stiffening, the Navaho then slumped and endeavored to feebly crawl off. Ponce ripped out his knife, pounced on the Navaho's chest, and finished their conflict with a thrust to the heart.

Ponce's temples pounded as he slowly rose. The fight had taken more out of him than it should have, and he stood there a few moments catching his breath. Then he remembered the Navaho's horse.

Whirling, Ponce shoved his knife into its sheath and ran to the patch of grass to retrieve his rifle. From there he jogged to the edge of the brush. Hundreds of yards to the west the dust cloud swirled. As yet, there was no sign of other warriors. He moved toward the Navaho's sorrel and reached for the dragging reins. The horse snorted, jerked its head away, and went to dash off. Ponce leaped, clutched the rope, and held on tight. His scent agitated the sorrel even more and he had to grip the reins with both hands to keep from being yanked off his feet.

Ponce had to quiet the horse quickly. He grabbed for its mane but the animal wrenched to the right and the reins nearly slipped from his grasp. Taking a short jump, he looped his right arm over the animal's neck and planted his feet firmly to show it who was the master. The sorrel, though, had ideas of its own and started to trot westward.

Ponce hauled on the horse's neck with all his might, causing the animal to veer into the brush. It went less than a dozen yards, then halted and tried to shake Ponce off. Since every moment of delay increased the danger, and since he already had more than enough horses to handle on the long ride to Sweet Grass, Ponce was in no frame of mind to go easy on the sorrel. He tried one last time to force it to stand still and failed.

Suddenly stepping back, Ponce whipped out his knife again and slit the animal's throat. The sorrel nickered as blood spewed from its throttle. It took a few steps toward the plain, then halted, wheezing noisily. Ponce slipped in close and opened the jugular groove with a deft slash. His forearms became sticky with crimson spray so he squatted and wiped them dry on the ground.

Standing, Ponce ran to where the Navaho had dropped the rifle. He looked back once and saw the sorrel sink to its front knees, its chest and legs a bright scarlet. It didn't take long to find the gun, and in short order Ponce was astride his horse and hastening eastward with the long string in tow.

Everything depended on how soon the war party realized one of its own had gone missing. Ponce pushed hard, heedless of the many sharp branches and leaves that tore at him and the animals. There was no time to think about erasing their tracks. He must put a lot of distance behind him.

The stolen stock slowed Ponce down but he wouldn't consider abandoning them. To Apaches horses were tokens of wealth; the more a man owned, the higher his public esteem. Ponce already had a sizeable herd thanks to the many raids led by Lickoyee-shis-inday, and before he quit the band he hoped to have twenty or more.

For the remainder of the day Ponce traveled across some of the most rugged country in Arizona. The searing heat had little effect on him but it readily tired the sweating horses. Twice he had to stop and beat flagging animals with sticks to keep them going.

Nightfall came and went. Ponce rode on until close to midnight. He would have gone longer but by then all the horses were flagging badly so he stopped in a sheltered ravine where there was grass for grazing. He took up a post on the rim and allowed himself to doze.

The first tinge of pink in the eastern sky found Ponce on horseback, hurrying to reach the Chiricahuas before the day was done.

The Dragoon and Chiricahua Mountains had long been the stronghold of the Chiricahua Apaches. Time and again they had expelled outsiders who dared to claim the land as their own. First it had been haughty Spaniards intent on educating the Apaches in the one true faith. Then it had been Mexicans, who came to mine for copper and other precious metals. Finally, the Apaches had clashed with relative newcomers to the region, the Americans, who asserted a right to the land because they had beaten the Mexicans in a great war.

Ponce would never accept the American claim. The Chiricahuas were his home. He'd rather fight and die, if need be, for the land that meant so much to him. Now he scoured the horizon with eager eyes for his first glimpse of the range he knew like he did the back of his hand. The mountains where he would be safe.

At the sanctuary known as Sweet Grass.

Chapter Seven

Clay Taggart's first impulse on seeing the cavalry escort was to vault erect and flee. He wouldn't have gotten five feet before the troopers spotted him, and realizing that, he did the next best thing. Picking up handfuls of dirt, he covered his legs and sprinkled some on his back. Then he put his head as close to the saguaro as he dared, tucked his arms close to its base, and went as rigid as a rock.

The buckboard moved at a snail's pace. Both occupants wore suits and bowlers. Beside them rode a captain in a dusty uniform who was listening to the older of the pair.

"—damned nice of you, Forester, to ride with us the rest of the way. Not that we'd need the protection. We haven't seen a lousy Apache the whole trip."

"That doesn't mean they're not around, Mr. Walters," the captain responded.

94

"Then why haven't they ambushed us?"

"If you had lived in Tucson longer, you'd know the answer," Captain Forester said. "Apaches only attack when it's in their best interests. Nine times out of ten they do it for the spoils." He gestured at the buckboard. "They don't have any use for wagons, so they'd likely figure the two of you weren't worth the bother."

"But wouldn't they want to lift our hair?"

"Not necessarily, sir," the officer said. "Apaches aren't like the Sioux and Cheyenne and other Plains tribes. They don't count coup, and as a rule they don't do much scalping. It has to do with their beliefs about the dead."

"I don't follow you," Walter said.

"Apaches want nothing to do with those who have died. When one of them passes on, right away the body is wrapped in a blanket and buried at a secret location, then all the deceased's belongings and wickiup are burned." Forester scratched at the stubble on his chin. "If a warrior takes a scalp, he has to go through a long purification process before he can keep it. Most think it's not worth the bother."

"Where did you learn so much about their heathen ways?"

"From the scouts at Fort Bowie. Some of them are Apache."

"I must say, I never thought when I left Illinois that—"

Distance and the rattle of accoutrements on the cavalry mounts prevented Clay from hearing the rest. He saw tired trooper after tired trooper go by, and only after the last quartet had disappeared to the east did he rise and rejoin the Chiricahuas.

Once across the road, Clay struck to the northwest. The band came on scattered ranches and gave them a wide berth. Occasionally, they encountered roving herds of cattle in which the Apaches showed no interest. They preferred horseflesh to beef and only resorted to stealing cows when there was a shortage of horses.

Clay couldn't wait to reach the spread of the man he was going to kill. He imagined the horrified look Jack Bitmer would wear when they came face to face, and relished the thought of making Bitmer's death an agonizing one. So distracted did he become by his daydreams that he didn't hear voices wafting over a hill to their left until Delgadito leaned over and slapped him on the arm to get his attention.

Instantly drawing rein, Clay cocked his head. The words were in English but too faint to make out. He handed his reins to Delgadito and went up the slope on foot, dropping prone near the crest.

Below lay a sprawling valley filled with everything from young calves to old bulls. A dozen cowboys were busy steer roping and branding. Clay had done the same countless times on his own ranch, and for a minute nostalgia provoked a deep sadness over the turn of events that had deprived him of the way of life he'd known and loved.

Some cowboys were born to the saddle. Others learned to cherish the work by becoming a puncher through circumstance. Whichever was the case, once they were a charter member of the cow crowd they'd rather die than do anything else for a living. Something about the feel of a dependable horse between a man's legs, about the creak and smell of saddle leather and the carefree life of the open range, got into a man's blood and never went away.

The yip of a puncher closing in on a running steer near the base of the hill caused Clay to duck down. He heard the thud of hoofs as the steer thundered up the slope with the cowhand on its tail. Scooting downward on his hands and knees, he rose just as the steer pounded over the top. The animal slanted to the right. And then came the cowboy, astonishment as plain as day on his face, reining up in alarm and giving voice to a bellow that must have been heard clear back to Tucson.

"Injuns! Injuns! Everybody, there's Injuns here!"

Clay had no desire to shoot the man. He turned to run as the puncher's hand dropped to a flashy Colt. A rifle cracked, and the cowboy tumbled backward.

Bounding like a jackrabbit, Clay reached the bottom and swung onto his horse. A chorus of incensed cries told him the rest of the hands were on the fly toward the hill, so without delay he reined the chestnut and galloped due south. The Apaches fell in behind him.

Clay looked back as the hands crested the hill. They hardly paused at the body. Palming their hardware and pulling out rifles, they flew after the band. Clay bent low, riding for his life, the wind whipping his hair. If he had his druthers, he'd rather be chased by the cavalry or other Indians or anyone except a passel of riled punchers. Cowboys were not only superb horsemen from having spent every day from dawn to dusk in the saddle, they were a lot more persistent than the army would be when one of their own bought the farm. They were pure hell with the hide off and as fearless as Apaches.

Scattered shots broke out, none drawing blood. Clay swept around another hill and rode like the wind across barren flatland, the Apaches staying even with him, the four of them forming a ragged line. Rifle fire fueled their flight. Clay glanced at the Chiricahuas and wondered what they were thinking.

At that moment, their thoughts were varied.

Fiero was filled with disgust at being made to run from a pack of lowly white-eyes. He was disappointed in Lickoyee-shis-inday, who had shown such promise in wiping out the poachers. He would much rather have dug in and fought. The odds meant nothing to him. Many times he'd faced far greater and survived.

Cuchillo Negro, on the other hand, approved highly of White Apache's leadership. True to Apache custom, he would rather run away to fight another day than let himself be senselessly slaughtered. His only complaint was that White Apache had been preoccupied the past few miles instead of fully alert as a *Shis-Inday* should be.

Delgadito had mixed feelings. He still didn't like being overshadowed by another, especially an *Americano*, but he no longer resented it so strongly. Not now that Cuchillo Negro had shown him the way to excite the entire Chiricahua nation into breaking the fetters of their white conquerors. All it would take was a series of successful raids, enough to convince his people that the White Apache was a man of powerful medicine. They would see a white-eye who was on their side, see that those who rode with him slew whites with impunity, and they would come to realize that Americans were not the invincible foes most Chiricahuas believed. More and more warriors would flock to join the band. Eventually they would drive the whites from their land, and when that was done, Delgadito would assume the leadership so long denied him and take his rightful place as war chief of the tribe.

Unaware of all this, Clay vaulted a narrow gully on the fly. While in midair a bullet tugged at his new hat. Several others buzzed close overhead. It seemed the cowboys were more interested in bringing him down than they were any of the warriors, and he knew why. Everyone in the territory had heard of the White Apache and of the bounty being offered for his corpse, no questions asked.

In an ironic switch, the Apaches rode silently while the cowboys whooped in bloodthirsty glee. None of the Chiricahuas wasted ammo by returning fire although several times Fiero began to lift his rifle as if to do so.

The open flatland gave way to a forest of saguaro that stretched for as far as the eye could see to the southwest. Clay would rather have run naked through a briar patch than attempt to lose the cowboys among the giant cactuses, but he had no choice. Into their midst he plunged, weaving and winding as openings presented themselves, doing his best to spare himself and the chestnut from harm where the saguaros were packed close together.

Slugs ripped into the cactus on either side, sending pieces flying. Something stung Clay's left cheek, cutting deep. A glance revealed the cowboys had fanned out to enter the saguaro at different points. Some were closer than others, and all were finding it hard to use their guns accurately with so many cactuses intervening.

Clay saw one puncher swing in behind him and cut loose with a pistol. The shots came much too close for comfort, so Clay shifted, leveling his Winchester. The cowboy panicked and slanted to the right, reining so abruptly his animal was unable to make the turn smoothly and plowed into a tall saguaro. Both squealed as they went down.

Other punchers were gaining ground too. Clay had to discourage them, so to that end he snapped off a swift volley that forced the cowboys to seek cover. Fiero joined in, but Delgadito and Cuchillo Negro held their fire.

For minutes the frenzied chase continued. The renegades held their own, riding flawlessly, at one with their mounts. All was going as well as could be expected until Delgadito's animal stepped into a hole.

Clay witnessed the spill out of the corner of an eye. He saw Delgadito leap clear as the animal went into a roll and heard the mount's tortured whinny as its foreleg shattered, the broken bone jutting through its skin. Since he was nearest, he skirted a wide saguaro to reach Delgadito before the cowboys did. He saw Delgadito rising unsteadily, saw a lean cowhand bearing down on the Apache and taking deliberate aim with a Winchester. Without giving a thought to the fact he was shooting a white man to save a redskin, he fired.

The cowhand sailed from the saddle with limbs outspread.

"Grab hold!" Clay shouted in Apache as he galloped up to Delgadito and lowered his left arm. Oddly, the warrior hesitated. And meanwhile, cowboys were converging from several directions at once.

Delgadito knew the *Americanos* were closing in on him. Yet he couldn't quite bring himself to reach for Lickoyee-shis-inday's hand knowing he would again owe his life to the white-eye. It was bad enough Taggart had saved him when the scalp hunters slaughtered his band; it was bad enough he had to live with the shame of having led his followers to their deaths. To be beholden once more to Taggart was like rubbing salt on a fresh wound. But a bullet clipping a cactus almost at his elbow reminded him he had to live in order to carry out his larger scheme to wreak vengeance on the *Americanos;* so, taking a short step, he leaped onto the chestnut behind White Apache.

Clay wheeled his mount and fled. He shoved his .44-40 at Delgadito, then palmed one of his ivory-handled Colts and banged two swift shots at the cowboys. With each shot a man fell. He faced front to devote his attention to riding and felt Delgadito lurch against him.

Fiero and Cuchillo Negro had slowed to allow them to catch up and were directing a withering hail of lead at the cowpokes, most of whom sought cover.

The chestnut struggled to maintain a full gallop bearing the weight of two men. Clay had to rein the horse in a little while keeping his eyes skinned for cowboys. He noticed several of the punchers were no longer pursuing and snapped off three more shots to discourage the remainder.

Gradually, one by one, the cowboys gave up, all except for a lanky pair who appeared determined to follow the Apaches to the gates of Hell, if need be. On the one hand Clay was annoyed by their persistence, but on the other he admired punchers who were so loyal to the brand they'd rather die than admit they'd been beaten.

A minute later even the last pair were forced to turn back when Fiero and Cuchillo Negro, their rifles reloaded, halted to steady their aim and cut loose with shots that clipped saguaros within inches of the cowboys. Reluctantly, the punchers turned around to rejoin their pards.

Clay was glad to see them go. He'd been riding with the Apaches for a while now but he still couldn't gun down men who were only doing their duty without feeling a pang of guilt. It wasn't like killing those who had tried to hang him, or those who wronged the Apaches.

Presently, the sea of saguaros ended. Chaparral provided cover, and Clay found a clearing among manzanitas where he reined up for the sake of their horses. He glanced over his shoulder and smiled at Delgadito. "That was a close one," he said in Apache before he realized Delgadito had his head bowed and saw that blood caked the warrior's shoulder and chest.

Sliding off, Clay turned just as the Apache pitched off toward him. He managed to get his arms out in time. Cuchillo Negro helped lower Delgadito to the ground.

The wound was high on the right side and still bleeding profusely. Clay had seen similar wounds before and knew they sometimes proved fatal. "We must help him," he said.

"I know a root that would do some good," Cuchillo Negro said, "but I do not know if I can find one quickly enough."

"Try," Clay said, and the warrior ran off. Clay looked up at Fiero. "We will need a small fire in case there are no roots. And I would like you to break open a cartridge so we can use the powder."

"Am I a woman that I should jump when another man tells me what to do?"

"No. You are Delgadito's friend and you want him to live."

Fiero sat there a full minute mulling what to do. He had agreed to let the *Americano* lead them, and he had on occasion helped the white man, such as the time he instructed Lickoyee-shis-inday in how to meet a formal challenge by another Chiricahua, but he wasn't one to take direct orders from anyone, not even another Apache.

Fiero gazed into Lickoyee-shis-inday's eyes and was surprised to see silent, sincere appeal. The thought struck him that this strange white-eye would probably do the same for him were he to be gravely wounded, a startling revelation. As Fiero saw it, whites and Apaches were inveterate enemies. Granted, Lickoyee-shis-inday had proven different from most of his kind, but the concept of a white man actually caring whether an Apache lived or died was virtually unthinkable. "Would you do the same for me?" he bluntly asked.

"Of course. We must always be ready to help one another. If we do not stick together, we will not last long."

The proposition needed a lot of thought. Fiero climbed down and walked into the trees, saying over a shoulder, "I will fetch wood for the fire."

"I am grateful," Clay said. With that problem taken care of, he studied the wound, gingerly probing around the bullet hole. The blood just wouldn't stop. He wondered if Delgadito would die, and what he should do in that case. The Apache stirred weakly. Clay shifted, his head lifting, and found the Apache's dark eyes regarding him with odd intensity.

"I will die soon, Lickoyee-shis-inday."

"You do not know that for certain," Clay responded. "It is not fitting for a man to talk of death when there is every chance he will live to be wrinkled with old age."

Delgadito gazed skyward. "An Apache knows when his time has come. This wound is worse than any other I have ever had. I can feel my insides growing wet with blood. They say when that happens there is no hope."

Alarmed by the news there was internal bleeding, Clay said brusquely, "Let me be the judge of whether you will pull through or not."

"Some things are beyond the control of men, and this is one of them," Delgadito said so softly the words were barely audible. "It is not for us to say if I will live." Sighing, he closed his eyes. "I do not mind telling you that I welcome death with a warm heart."

Exasperated, Clay switched to English. "How the dickens can you say such nonsense, pard? Life is too damned precious for us to chuck it aside without putting up a fight."

"I tired, White Apache," Delgadito said, and moved an arm enough to touch a finger to his chest. "In here."

"You're talking craziness."

Delgadito was fast losing consciousness. He spoke once more in his own tongue. "When the white-eyes took our freedom, they took our life. Those on the reservation are already dead but do not yet realize it." He coughed and his voice dropped even more. "It is better that I die now, before the *Shis-Inday* are no more."

"Don't give up the ghost yet," Clay said in English. He remembered hearing somewhere that it was best to keep people in Delgadito's condition awake and talking, so he went on, "If there's anyone who knows about taking the big jump, it's me. I was guest of honor at a string party, after all. But I didn't go meekly, and that's one of the reasons I'm still kicking. You've got to do the same. Like me, you have something to live for." Clay's features hardened. "I've got a no-account snake in the grass to settle with, and you have a whole passel of white-eyes to deal with."

Quick Killer

Clay stopped on seeing that the warrior was unconscious again. Since there was nothing else he could do until the others returned, he slipped a rifle bullet from his bandoleer and drew his butcher knife. Prying the cartridge open took a while, but at length he poured the small amount of gunpowder it contained onto a flat rock.

Fiero showed up with an armful of wood and soon had a fire going. Not long after Cuchillo Negro returned to report no luck in finding the type of root he needed in order to make a poultice.

"Then we do this the hard way," Clay said.

The flow of blood had reduced to a trickle. Clay slowly sprinkled grains of gunpowder around the edges of the wound, then lightly pried the wound further apart and fed grains into the hole. He had to be careful not to use too much or the cure would prove instantly fatal.

Fiero and Cuchillo Negro watched without commenting. It was Apache custom for warriors to hold their own counsel when they had nothing worthwhile to say. Both wanted their former leader to live, but both also knew his fate was in the hands of *Yusn*.

Clay wished there was water nearby so he could wash the wound beforehand. As a substitute, he ripped off a small piece of his shirt, moistened it with spittle, and wiped off as much excess blood as the material would absorb. Then, tossing the cloth aside, he selected a slender firebrand and lifted it from the fire. Tiny flames licked at the air as he lowered the lit end close to the bullet hole.

Delagdito stirred but did not awaken.

"Here goes nothing," Clay said to himself, and dipped the burning tip. Immediately the gunpowder caught. There was a blinding flash and flames shot

105

from the hole. The acrid scent of smoke and charred flesh filled the air.

Delgadito's dark eyes snapped wide, reflecting acute torment. He tried to sit up but couldn't. Raising his head, he stared at the smoke pouring from the wound, then at Clay. His mouth parted as if he were going to speak.

"I did the only thing I could," Clay said in his defense.

Eyelids fluttering, the tall warrior collapsed and lay insensate, his chest rising and falling.

Blood had stopped flowing from the hole. Clay eased a fingertip into it to ascertain whether the internal bleeding had likewise ceased. The flesh was a sickly black for over an inch deep. Underneath it was brown except at the bottom where it was a healthy pink. He found no trace of fresh blood.

"Do we go now, White Apache?" Fiero asked.

Clay could not quite believe his ears. "Go?"

"Yes. To kill the white-eye who is your enemy."

"And what about Delgadito?"

"We have done all we can for him."

"But he is too weak to move. We must stay the night to watch over him. In the morning we will head back to Sweet Grass."

"We will not go through with the raid?"

"No. We dare not leave Delgadito here alone. He cannot fend for himself. We will take him back to Sweet Grass where he can heal in peace."

Never in Fiero's experience had he heard of an attack being called off simply because a lone warrior had been hurt. Once, he would have objected strenuously to being denied his share of possible plunder because of the misfortunes of another. Apaches looked out for themselves. That was the essential creed by which they all lived, the acknowledged law under which they had existed since time immemorial. Yet here was this White Apache telling them that they must regard the welfare of other warriors as they would their own. It was an idea that would take considerable time to accept, if ever.

Cuchillo Negro had risen. "We will do as you say, White Apache. I will see to the horses."

"And I will hunt game for our supper," Fiero declared.

Watching them walk off, Clay smiled. Something told him he had won another round in his campaign to win them over to his way of thinking. Provided all went well, before long they'd be his to command as he pleased, and then Arizona would run red with the blood of those who had wronged him!

Chapter Eight

The young Chiricahua called Ponce arrived at Sweet Grass as twilight descended on the remote retreat. After setting the horses free to graze, he rode to the gurgling stream and squatted to drink. As his hand dipped into the cool water, his eyes drifted to a fresh set of tracks in the soft soil nearby. He immediately stiffened and glanced suspiciously around.

Apaches were masterful trackers. From an early age they were instructed in the art, taught by the very best warriors. So skillful were they, their ability was considered by many to border on the supernatural, an illusion the Apaches did all they could to foster.

Warriors learned, for instance, that when the toes of tracks pointed inward, then the prints had been made by Indians, and when the toes pointed outward, then white-eyes or the *Nakai-hey* were responsible. From the depth of tracks and the strides taken, Apaches could tell the approximate weight and height of those who made them. They were also versed in the many styles of footwear, from moccasins to boots to sandals.

So it was that the instant Ponce set eyes on the fresh prints he knew they had been made by someone wearing Apache moccasins. Since the other renegades were off on the raid, he knew it couldn't have been one of them. And since it was rare for reservation warriors who had accepted the white yoke to come to Sweet Grass, he immediately assumed the footprints had been made by another Army scout sent to ferret out the band.

Rising, Ponce scoured the stream and was confounded to see another set of fresh tracks, this time a trail left by a woman. His blood quickened as he hunkered down to examine them, for they were of a size and shape he knew as well as he knew his own. Yet they could have been made by any woman the same age, he reasoned, and stilled the alarm blaring in his breast.

The tracks led northward toward the rugged heights dominating Sweet Grass. Ponce levered a round into the chamber of his rifle and set off on the trail at a dog trot. Because he was following fellow Apaches, he took more precautions than he would have had he been following whites. Like a flitting specter he covered the rough ground, never still in one spot for more than a second at a time, never exposing himself for even the briefest of moments. Totally silent, he pressed upward until he came to a stand of ponderosa, and here he paused behind a wide trunk to adjust his mind to the rhythm of the woodland.

Somewhere to the east a squirrel chattered, to the west sparrows chirped gaily.

Ponce gazed up the mountain slope, a slope he was very familiar with from the many times he had explored it in search of game for their meals. Above the timber reared clusters of jumbled boulders, a maze few could negotiate. He couldn't imagine the couple going there.

Ponce was perplexed by the couple's presence. It made no sense for a scout to have brought a woman to Sweet Grass. Nor did it make sense for a reservation warrior to have done so. Apache women were every bit as hardy as their men and equally capable of living off the land, but women weren't permitted to take part in warfare. There were exceptions, of course, but they were rare.

Believing his quarry to be among the tall pines, Ponce advanced slowly. He was quite surprised when the tracks led straight through the trees to the rocky elevation beyond. From the base of the lowest boulder he swept the cluttered boulder field without spying anyone.

Ponce was about to go on when one of the woman's tracks arrested his attention. Marking the bare earth beside it were dozens of dark drops. Ponce touched one with a fingertip and sniffed his finger. It was blood, as he knew it would be. He took another step, saw where the woman had stumbled to one knee, and then spotted a severed finger lying close by.

Ponce stared at it, at the trickle of blood still oozing from the pink flesh, and felt an icy, invisible finger scrape the length of his spine. Quickening his pace, he went another fifty yards and came on the second finger. Like the other, it had been cut off mere minutes ago.

They were markers, Ponce realized, deliberately left for him to find. He ran now, recklessly, winding among the boulders until he came on a small cleared space and there in the center, wedged upright in the soil, was a third finger.

Halting, Ponce raised the finger to his nose and inhaled. His jaw muscles twitched and he flushed scarlet. He darted behind a rock monolith and gently set the finger down. Then he sprinted onward, sheer rage filling him with blood lust so intense he could hardly think straight.

Two more fingers were found before Ponce reached the crest of a ridge. The twilight had deepened to near complete darkness and it was difficult for him to see the tracks. Often he had to feel the ground for the telltale impressions.

Once past the ridge, the slope steepened sharply. Ponce climbed in an awkward crouch, his pace reduced to a virtual crawl. A flat shelf afforded a place to ease the cramps in his calves. He saw a large flat rock in front of him, and on top of it the vague outline of something foreign. Only when he bent down did he make out the outline of a human foot, a woman's foot, sheared off at the ankle by a razor-sharp tomahawk.

The blood trail was a black ribbon leading ever upward. Ponce climbed on, the scent so strong he no longer had to bother finding footprints. He seemed to remember there being a clearing on top of the next slope, and there was. But the figure spread-eagled in the middle was a new addition.

Ponce ran to her, blood thundering in his ears. He'd done more than his share of torturing Mexicans and *Americanos* in his time, and had seen the gruesome handiwork of those who hunted his people, but those experiences did little to prepare him for the shock of seeing the woman he cared for butchered and dying.

Ko-do's eyes, ears, and nose were gone. Her left hand was a stump, her right leg ended at the ankle. Strips of skin were missing from her neck and arms. She breathed in feeble gasps, her body trembling. Looped around her neck was a length of rope.

Ponce knelt and touched her forehead. Ko-do flinched, shuddered more violently, then whined. "It is I," he said softly.

Somehow she found the strength to speak in a strangled whisper. "I am sorry. I told him where to find you."

"Who?"

"Tats-ah-das-ay-go."

"I will cut out his heart," Ponce vowed, running his finger across her brow.

"For my sake, do not fight him."

"You know better."

Ko-do's breathing slowed. For the longest while she made no comment. Then, "What are you waiting for?"

"It is a hard thing for a man to do."

"Please."

"He will hear."

"He already knows."

"I will miss you, Firefly."

"And I you." Ko-do convulsed briefly. "Please. Do it now. For me."

Without hesitation, Ponce placed the muzzle of his Winchester against her temple and stroked the trigger. As the blast echoed off across the valley he wheeled and darted into the boulders. He expected an answering shot, but there was none.

Anyone other than an Apache might have broken down at that point, might have succumbed to shock or tears or sorrow so profound it numbed body and soul. Ponce did not. He had been bred since infancy

112

to control his feelings, to bend his emotions to the iron rod of his will, to achieve a state of complete self-mastery. So although inwardly profound sadness mixed with a raging thirst for revenge dominated him, he neither showed it in his expression nor allowed the upheaval to cloud his mind. He knew his judgment must be unimpaired if he was to stand any chance at all of beating the notorious Quick Killer.

Ponce listened, but heard nothing. He looked, but saw no one. Yet as sure as the moon was rising in the east, Tats-ah-das-ay-go was out there somewhere, waiting to slay him at an opportune moment.

Every Apache had heard of Quick Killer, the Army scout who rubbed out renegades for the price of a good horse. Yet Quick Killer's chosen line of work wasn't held against him. Many warriors would have liked to do the same but weren't as skilled at tracking or killing.

Several times Ponce had heard Delgadito mention that one day the white-eyes would send Quick Killer against them, most recently after Nah-kah-yen tried to wipe out their band. According to Delgadito, Tats-ah-das-ay-go was twice as good as Nah-kah-yen. Clever, tough, and as swift as lightning, Quick Killer was more to be dreaded than the whole *Americano* Army.

Knowing this, Ponce didn't hesitate. He was going to avenge Ko-do's death, come what may. In that respect, he was no different from all men everywhere. No man would ever sit idly by when their loved ones were threatened or slain. They will do what has to be done regardless of the consequences.

Ponce moved among the boulders with catlike speed and silence, senses alert for his enemy. He suspected that Quick Killer was aware of his movements and mystified because the scout didn't attack, especially after all the trouble Quick Killer had gone to in order to lure him to the spot.

The breeze picked up, as it often did at that time of the night, the fluttering whisper of its passage loud enough to drown out faint noises. Ponce turned this way and that as he sought his quarry, never rising higher than a low crouch, his cocked rifle clenched firmly.

Presently Ponce came to a cleared space and went to dart across it. He took a single step when a rifle boomed to his left and his right leg was jarred out from under him by a jolting blow. On elbows and knees he scrambled for cover, then took stock. He didn't return fire even though he knew the scout had moved after pulling the trigger and he had a fair idea where Quick Killer was now concealed. Any Apache would have done the same.

The bullet had caught Ponce in the fleshy part of the thigh and bored a neat hole clean through. There was scant blood and the bone hadn't been broken, so Ponce considered himself extremely lucky.

Crawling, Ponce bore to the right. He tried putting himself in Quick Killer's moccasins and decided the scout's next move would be to circle around and come at him from the opposite direction. Only he would be waiting. Once Delgadito and the rest saw Quick Killer's body, they would regard him with greater respect than had been their custom to date. Ponce could hardly wait.

The second rifle shot sounded much closer. Ponce jerked his head back as dirt spewed into his face, then he rolled against the base of a boulder where the deep shadow screened him. He touched his cheek and felt blood. By the width of a finger had his life been spared.

Quick Killer

Ponce didn't move for the longest while. He wanted Quick Killer to believe he was on the go, so every so often he picked up tiny pebbles and hurled them as far as he could. It was an old trick but one that often worked.

At last Ponce ventured out among the boulders. Here they were much larger, jagged monoliths squatting somber and black in the darkness. He made no noise on the hard ground, and he was confident he would soon have Quick Killer in his sights.

A sudden shout surprised Ponce and he turned toward its source, scraping a forearm on the soil as he did.

"Make this easy on yourself, young one. Give up and I will grant you a painless death."

Ponce thought he saw a vague form. He snapped off two shots and heard a mocking laugh that wavered eerily on the wind. Clearly he had missed, and he was ashamed for having fired without a definite target. It had been the wrong thing to do. Now Quick Killer had him pinpointed precisely.

Rolling to the left, Ponce pushed up and limped rapidly southward. He had a troublesome thought. It appeared that the scout was toying with him, treating him as if he were a mere boy and not a man. For Quick Killer to call out that way had been an insult. No warrior would dare do such a thing when fighting a foe worthy of the name.

Ponce didn't like being rated as of little regard. He had slain dozens since taking the renegade trail, and on forays into Mexico had held his own with the likes of Fiero and Cuchillo Negro. He deserved to be treated with caution, not contempt.

Briefly, the wind died, and Ponce paused so as not to give himself away. He scanned the vicinity without result, then moved on when the wind resumed. Due to his single-minded devotion to the matter at hand, he didn't realize he was near the spot where the maiden lay until he saw the outline of her body. The sight brought an odd constriction to his throat and he swallowed hard.

Ponce should have gone around. He should have stayed among the boulders to avoid detection. But he wanted one last glimpse of Firefly before going down the slope, so he dashed into the open past her. Too late, it registered that her body was much larger than it should be. Too late, he saw that the figure on the ground wore a buckskin shirt and leggings and not a beaded dress. And too late, Ponce tried to level his Winchester.

Quick Killer was a blur as he shifted and swung a sturdy leg, striking the younger warrior across the back of both feet to bring Ponce crashing down. Desperately, Ponce tried to brace a hand and rise to his knees but something smashed him in the temple and the next thing he knew he was flat on his side tasting dirt in his mouth as the barrel of a rifle was jammed against his ear.

"Do not move, young one, or you will die much sooner than you have to."

The tone was that of steel grinding on steel, of ice made into sound. Ponce did as he was told, but not out of fear. Every moment he was spared was another moment he might turn the tables and avenge Ko-do.

"You have talent, young one," Quick Killer said. "Were you to live another five winters, you would be one of the best."

"You did not need to involve the girl," Ponce said as a rough hand roamed his body searching for concealed weapons.

Quick Killer

"A wise hunter always uses the right bait to lure his prey into his snare."

"When hunting animals, yes."

"And since when is hunting men any different?" Quick Killer said. "Can it be that you have rode with Delgadito for so long and learned so little? Trickery is the Apache way, and has always been so. What we lack in numbers, we make up for with our wits. How else have we survived so long?"

Ponce was flipped onto his back. He couldn't very well refute the truth, so he made no comment.

"Where are the others?"

"I do not know," Ponce lied, and had to bite his lower lip to keep from crying out when the scout rammed a foot into his thigh wound.

"If you want the same treatment as your woman, I will not hesitate to cut you up. But I should think you would be smarter than she was."

"I am not afraid to die!"

"Then you are a worthy Chiricahua," Quick Killer said, the corners of his mouth twitching upward.

"Do you mock me, breed?" Ponce snapped. He never saw the blow that rendered him unconscious. When next he opened his eyes, he was flat on his back beside a small fire, his arms and legs bound. His head ached abominably. Twisting his neck, he discovered the scout had toted him to the valley floor and they were now camped a few yards from the stream. Tats-ah-das-ay-go was skinning a bloody rabbit.

"You have much to learn, cub," the scout said without looking up.

"How did you know I had revived?" Ponce asked, forcing his sluggish brain and mouth to work despite the terrible agony pounding in his temples.

"The rhythm of your breathing changed," Quick Killer disclosed. "It will give a man away every time."

"You must think you are crafty, like a fox," Ponce said scornfully.

"No, I know I am smarter than most," the other countered. "Otherwise my enemies would have killed me long ago." He cut off chunks of dripping meat and began impaling them on a slender stick he had whittled to a sharp point. "You, however, must be a weak thinker or you would not have let yourself be taken so easily."

"Save your insults, breed."

This time Quick Killer spun, the makeshift spit pointed at the young warrior's face. "Are you so stupid that you failed to learn your lesson the last time?" He sighed. "Respect, stripling. It is all that really matters in this life. When a man has earned it, he can hold his head high. Without it, he is as a lowly worm." Quick Killer resumed placing meat on the stick. "Surely I have earned yours."

"You dream with your eyes open."

"Delgadito would not be so childish," Quick Killer said. "He would be man enough to admit he had met his match."

"You?" Ponce said. "You flatter yourself, Tats-ah-das-ay-go. Delgadito is a better warrior than you will ever be. He has proven his ability time and again. None are his equal." Ponce coiled his legs and sat up, the effort aggravating the torment in his head. "Certainly not a man like you, who makes much of respect but who has earned only contempt by working for the white dogs who want to exterminate our kind."

"We do what we have to."

Ponce secretly tested the rope binding his wrists while saying, "No one made you a scout against your will. You went to the whites of your own accord and asked if you could work for them. And why? To kill for money." He adopted a haughty sneer. "When a man runs with dogs, what does that make him?"

Quick Killer jabbed the bottom of the stick into the ground so that the meat hung at an angle over the low flames. "You have a talent for insulting others," he remarked. "If I did not need you alive, I would slit your throat right now."

"Why have you spared me?"

"For the same reason I kept your woman alive after taking her from her village. To use as bait."

Ponce didn't like the sound of that. "To catch Delgadito? Do you really think he will fall into your clutches as easily as I did?"

"I have no intention of going to all the trouble of taking him alive," Quick Killer said. "All I need to do is lure him within rifle range, and for that you will serve most admirably."

"You are wrong if you think Delgadito would risk his life for mine," Ponce said, but he was not as sure as he tried to sound. "And besides, he will not be alone. There are twelve warriors in our band, more than you can fight alone."

"Twelve?" Quick Killer chuckled. "You speak with two tongues, young one. I read the sign in this valley most carefully when I arrived. There are five of you counting the one called White Apache."

"You are guessing," Ponce bluffed.

"Tracks do not lie. And they tell me that five different men have lived in this valley for some time. Four walk like Apaches, with light treads and short steps. One clomps about like a white-eye even though he wears Apache moccasins. He also drinks like a white-eye, by kneeling beside the stream instead of squatting as a true warrior would do."

"So you know, then," Ponce conceded. "But you are still outnumbered. Even if you should slay Delgadito, the others will stop you from collecting your blood money."

"Only if I fail to kill them first."

The insight startled the youth. "Delgadito is not the only one you are after?"

"No. I want him and the White Apache most of all," Quick Killer said. "But since long ago I learned not to leave a job half finished, I will kill the rest to prevent them from coming after me later."

Ponce offered one last argument. "Nah-kah-yen tried and lost his life. You would do well to learn from his mistakes."

"The only mistake he made was in thinking he was good enough to handle Delgadito." Quick Killer adjusted the stick to roast the meat more evenly. "A man who oversteps himself often falls flat on his face."

"As you will," Ponce predicted. He had given up on the ropes. They were tied too tight, the knots too secure. Yet somehow he must break loose or else find a way of alerting his friends when they arrived at the sanctuary.

The scout eased his hunting knife from its sheath and held the blade so that it reflected the firelight. "You might like to know that your woman was very brave. I had to remove both of her eyes before she told me where to find you."

The reminder provoked Ponce into attempting an awkward lunge. He wanted to knock Quick Killer into the fire but was swatted down instead.

"Behave, cub. Your time will come soon enough."

"So will yours. I just wish I could be there to see it." Ponce lay on his side, reflecting. He had one thing in his favor. Delgadito and the others wouldn't return for days, perhaps a week or more if they stole a lot of horses and had to go out of their way to evade cavalry patrols on their way back. In that event, the scout might lose interest and wander elsewhere. Or so he hoped until the next statement Quick Killer uttered.

"You have no idea how much killing Delgadito and the White Apache means to me. No matter how long it takes, no matter what I have to do, I will bring them back. And then everyone, whites and Indians alike, will look on Tats-ah-das-ah-go with the respect he deserves."

Chapter Nine

Delgadito appeared to be dying. His breaths were irregular and labored. His body quivered in convulsive bursts that made his breathing worse. The wound had discolored to an ugly black and blue, the flesh festering in a pus-filled sore.

Clay Taggart looked down on the pale warrior and made a critical decision. "There is a ranch over those hills to the south. I will go there and see if they have what we need to help him."

"Is that wise?" Fiero asked, remembering the last time Lickoyee-shis-inday had visited his own kind. "They will kill you on sight."

"I must do something," Clay said, partly out of concern for the warrior who had saved his neck from being stretched and partly because he suspected the others wouldn't help him in his vendetta against Miles Gillett without Delgadito there to goad

122

them along. Hitching at his gunbelt, he stepped to the chestnut and swung up.

Cuchillo Negro came over. "We will wait until sunrise. No longer. The patrol we saw this morning might double back and find our trail."

"I understand," Clay said.

It had been two days since they tangled with the cowboys, yet they had gone less than twenty miles. In addition to Delgadito's condition slowing them down, they had to contend with a column of troopers that had arrived in the area with remarkable dispatch. Clay guessed they were the same bunch he'd run into at the road. They were conducting a thorough sweep that would eventually uncover the hiding place he'd picked deep in the chaparral if the band didn't move on soon. Say, by first light.

Clay rode with the cocked .44-40 in his right hand. He made a point of sticking to ground covered by grass and brush so as not to raise any dust. To his best recollection, the ranch he intended to visit was owned by a man named Welch, a devout transplanted Kentucky miner who had come West for his health and been able to build a thriving cattle herd. Clay had only met the man twice and visited the house but once, briefly. At that time, Welch had four hired hands.

On the lookout for punchers, Clay was puzzled when he spotted shimmering pinpoints of bright light along the bottom of the foremost hill. As he drew near the pinpoints resolved into shiny strands supported by regularly spaced posts.

"I'll be damned," Clay muttered. "Thorny fence." Or barbed wire, as some called it. A few ranchers had imported rolls of the stuff and drawn the wrath of their own neighbors for their audacity. Several had come to blows. And there were some who claimed worse trouble loomed on the horizon, that one day violence would erupt between those who reckoned they had the right to hem in their own property if they so desired and those who equated rangeland with wide open spaces.

The immediate problem Clay faced was getting onto the ranch. A fine jumper could clear the fence in a single hurdle, but he had no idea whether the chestnut was capable of doing so and he wasn't about to lose the horse on a gamble. Dismounting, he applied his Bowie to the top strand, in reality, a pair of thick wires wound together with keen spikes at intervals. He cut and scraped and dug slowly into the metal. In the process he was also dulling the edge on his knife, which he couldn't abide.

Clay rode westward, seeking a gap or break. He came to a draw where the wire had been strung about two feet off the bottom, not high enough for a cow to pass under but more than enough space for him to slide through. Tying the chestnut to a post, he proceeded on foot.

The afternoon sun beat down mercilessly. Twice Clay spooked lizards that darted off at astounding speed. To the east grazed cattle. To the west the grassland was replaced by mesquite.

It struck Clay as downright strange that here he was, a man who had once hated Apaches, risking his life to save one. And not just any old redskin. He was helping the most feared renegade in all of Arizona. Which proved that random circumstance had more sway in a fellow's life than all the good intentions in the world.

The hills were few. Beyond lay more grass, more cattle. A mile off stood the ranch house, stable, bunkhouse and corral. Clay saw no riders but left nothing to chance. He approached the ranch as he would a military post, with the utmost care. His training in Apache ways served him in good stead and presently he was secreted in shrubbery adjacent to the stable.

From the house wafted the merry tinkle of a piano and voices raised in harmonious song. Five buckboards were parked close to the hitching post. In the corral a pair of punchers were breaking a horse.

The peaceful scene tugged at Clay's heartstrings. Once again he was reminded of the rough but rewarding life he had forsaken for the sake of vengeance. Once again he longed to return to the old days, and his resolve faltered. But not for long because a striking, massive figure in an expensive suit appeared at the front window on the ground floor, a man endowed with a powerful frame so distinctive it could only belong to the man Clay longed to repay for the vile injustice done him: It was none other than Miles Gillett.

Clay was so amazed he forgot to use his rifle, and then Gillett strode back into the room. Clay flattened and wormed closer to the window. Apparently, Welch was having a get-together of some sort and had invited a number of friends and acquaintances. Where Gillett fit in, Clay had no idea. So far as he knew, Miles and Welch had never been very close. They'd always moved in different social circles.

Once abreast of the window, Clay saw many people moving about within. Blinding glare kept him from distinguishing features. He tucked the Winchester to his shoulder but held his fire, waiting for Gillett to reappear. He would only get one chance so he must make his shots count.

The singing went on and on, punctuated by loud conversations and much laughter. The guests were having a grand old time. Clay saw two people approach the window and tensed, thinking his time had come. They were women, however, and the sight of one sent a shiver down his spine.

Lilly Gillett was as ravishing as ever. Vivid images and sensations swamped over Clay; of the softness and scent of her luxuriant hair, the swell of her full breasts under his palms, the exquisite sweetness of her rosy lips on his. Lilly was the love of his life, the woman he'd yearned to marry, the radiant angel he'd set on a pedestal only to learn the hard way that her halo hid a set of devilish horns. For Lilly was the woman who had betrayed his love, who had played him for a fool so that Miles could steal his land. Next to her husband, she was the most treacherous, conniving creature in all of creation.

Automatically, Clay sighted on her chest. He'd never shot a woman before but at that particular instant he was ready and willing. Only a red haze shrouded his vision and his hands began shaking uncontrollably. He willed himself to relax, steeled his nerves, and smiled as the haze slowly faded.

Lilly and the other woman were gone.

Clay bided his time, hardly noticing the downward arc of the sun and the lengthening shadows cast by the oak trees in the front yard. The barking of a dog somewhere out back didn't disturb him either. Revenge was within his grasp and he wouldn't be denied.

The day was nearly done when the door opened and out bustled the guests. There were more women than men, and each and every one had to share a fond farewell with Welch's wife, who held the reason for the festivities bundled in swaddling in her arms. The women made quite a fuss over the infant, touching and kissing and hugging it as if it were their very own.

Quick Killer

Clay had eyes only for Miles and Lilly Gillett. The wealthy couple were at the center of the crowd, talking to another husband and wife. Try as he might, Clay was unable to get a clear shot. When everyone moved in a body toward the buggies, he lowered his rifle and crawled to the left for a better shot. The new angle permitted him to see more of Miles and Lilly, but not enough to guarantee a kill.

Momentarily, the advancing ranks parted. Clay elevated the .44-40 and fixed a bead on the chest of his nemesis, but no sooner had he done so than the ranks closed again and he was denied the opportunity. He saw Lilly doting over the baby and thought of their own once cherished plan to have children some day, a plan ruined when Miles Gillett came between them. As a result, Clay would never know what it was like to take a stroll with a waddling little son at his side. He'd never know the joy of teaching his offspring to fish and hunt and ride and do the thousand and one things a man had to know to be worthy of the brand.

Clay aimed at the middle of the guests, his sinews as tightly strung as the barbed wire he'd seen before. His trigger finger was rock steady. All he needed was an unobstructed view for a mere second or two.

A heavyset woman with gray hair walked in front of Gillett, her bulk blocking him from eyebrows to toes. Clay saw her begin to turn, to lumber toward a nearby buckboard, and he lightly curved his finger on the trigger. He was on the verge of firing when harsh snarling broke out very close at hand and he twisted to see a large black cur bearing down on him with its lips curled up over its gleaming teeth.

Clay spun, leveling the Winchester just as the mongrel sprang. The boom of the retort rocked his eardrums as the heavy caliber slug ripped into the dog's forehead, then exploded out the rear of its cranium. The mongrel slammed to the grass, sliding to within inches of Clay's moccasins. At the buckboards women were calling out, demanding to know what was going on, while some of the men stared suspiciously at the shrubbery. From the stable ran several punchers, unlimbering hardware.

As yet no one had spotted Clay. He dived and snaked toward the corral, keeping one eye on the guests and another on the cowhands. Welch was moving toward them, asking if they knew who had fired the shot.

Suddenly a short incline appeared. Clasping the rifle to his side, Clay rolled down to the corral and crouched beside a post. Rather than try to flee across open pasture, he dashed to the corner of the stable, checked to verify no one was by the open doors, and scooted within. A ladder brought him to a loft. He cracked the hay door so he could keep track of events and saw Welch and the three punchers moving toward the shrubbery, the hired hands with their six-shooters cocked.

"What is it, Arthur?" called out Mrs. Welch, her babe clutched protectively to her breast.

"We don't know yet, Ethel," answered Welch. He was about to squeeze through the row of bushes but a lanky puncher tugged at his jacket sleeve.

"Let me, boss," the man said, and went first, squeezing through to the other side. On spotting the dog, he dropped into a squat and pivoted right and left. "It's Buck!" he said. "He's been shot."

Welch and the other two men joined the lanky hand. They examined the mongrel, then straightened and scoured the area. From where Clay perched, he could just hear their voices.

128

"What do you think happened?" Welch asked no one in particular. "Who would shoot a good dog and run off?"

"Injuns," said the lanky one.

"Apaches, most likely," chimed in another.

"But why?" Welch replied. "It makes no sense, not even for those heathens."

"Apaches don't need an excuse to kill," declared the last cowpoke. "They do it for the thrill. I'd wager a month's pay that some wanderin' buck snuck in close for a look-see at the spread and had to gun down old Buck when the dog caught his damned scent."

"If so, where is the buck now?" Welch wondered.

The lanky cowboy wagged his shooting iron. "Me and the boys will poke around some, Mr. Welch."

"Thank you, Larry." Welch glanced at his visitors. "Under the circumstances it might be wise for me to have everyone go back into the house until the coast is clear. Let me know if you find anything."

"Sure thing, boss."

Clay watched Welch shoo the women indoors. The husbands, however, were eager to help in the hunt, and presently there were upwards of a dozen armed men prowling around the yard and the corral and moving out across the fields. Miles Gillett was one of them.

At long last Clay had the clear shot he wanted, yet now that he'd had a while to ponder on the situation, he refrained. Four men were in front of the stable, more on the sides. He knew he wouldn't live five minutes once he gave his position away. And as much as he craved vengeance, he craved life more. He had to live in order to mete out justice to the members of the posse that had done Gillett's dirty work.

Larry and another cowpoke were directly below the hay doors. The lanky puncher gestured at the stable and said, "I reckon it won't hurt to look in there."

"No Injun in his right mind would trap himself inside a building," said his companion.

"You never know," was Larry's argument. Together they entered, their spurs jingling lightly.

Clay lost sight of them as they moved below him. Outside, two more men came toward the corral, and he debated whether to fight or flee if he were discovered.

"No one in the stalls," said the companion.

"Same with the tack room," Larry stated.

"What about the loft?"

Clay slid to the right and furiously scooped with both hands. There were no bales to hide behind but there was plenty of loose hay, and in moments he had covered himself completely. He glimpsed the ladder, saw it jiggle as someone climbed. Larry's white Stetson materialized and the cowhand gave the loft a once-over. Clay could see the puncher's dark eyes narrow as they roved over the spot where he lay.

"Anything?" asked the man below.

"I don't rightly know yet," Larry said, coming higher. He set a boot on the hay and was lifting his hog-leg when a gunshot thundered to the west.

Clay was glad when the lanky puncher went lickety-split down from the loft and rushed from the stable to investigate. Shoving off the hay, he descended and ran to the back door. He spied several men running westward. Everyone was converging in that direction, so without delay he sprinted to the front, slipped along the corral to the shrubbery, and crouch-walked to the edge of the grass to the south.

In the distance was the mouth of the draw. So near, yet too far. He decided to wait for dark before moving from cover.

Folding his forearms under his chin, Clay made himself comfortable, pulled his hat low, and let his mind drift. The searchers had already been through the shrubbery from end to end so he felt safe staying there. He didn't count on having to deal with another dog.

Loud sniffing alerted him. Clay raised his head and peered through the bushes at four slim white legs moving along the next row over. It was smaller than the mongrel, a house-bred canine, he guessed. Mrs. Welch's pet, out relieving itself.

The dog came to Buck and circled the body three times, becoming more and more excited by the scent of blood. Moving in ever widening circles, the dog abruptly scampered toward the stable but drew up short less than six feet from Clay. He identified it as a Highland Terrier, a Scottish breed fancied by the well-to-do and noted for their courage and fighting ability. The last thing he needed was for the terrier to find him, yet it did.

Clay rose to his knees as the dog's strident yipping carried on the breeze. Everyone would hear. The animal danced this way and that, staying well beyond his reach, glaring and barking and snapping. Since someone was bound to come, Clay bent at the waist and sped off toward the draw.

The Highland Terrier advanced to the grass but would go no further. A bundle of energy, it bounced like a shaggy ball and continued to yowl madly.

Shouts signified people were hastening to the scene. Clay spotted a trio jogging past the stable but fortunately none were looking his way. He covered fifteen yards, then twenty. At thirty he straightened and raced like the wind.

"Lookee there! An Injun!"

Rifles cracked. Bullets thudded into the ground or whizzed past. Clay weaved to make it harder for them. Five or six men were in swift pursuit while others were hurrying to the corral for mounts.

Clay flew as if his ankles were endowed with wings. The grueling months spent among the Chiricahuas, hardening his body as it had never been hardened before, paid dividends now, enabling him to pull ahead of those on foot. Several slacked off, realizing they could never catch him.

The horsemen were a whole different problem. Two riders shot from the corral, a third from the stable, and opened fired as soon as they cleared the shrubbery. One was Larry.

Clay had to discourage them. Wheeling, he snapped off a shot that missed but caused them to swerve wide and bought him another twenty-five yards. In the meantime, women poured from the house and commenced cheering the riders on.

A full-blooded Apache would have proven a challenge for the horsemen to overtake. Apaches were incredibly fast over short distances, able to hold their own against ordinary mounts. Small wonder, since it wasn't uncommon for warriors to travel seventy miles in a single day and never stop to rest.

Clay wished he could do the same. A few more months, perhaps, and he would be that capable, but he wouldn't live a few more minutes if he didn't think of a means of escaping. The pounding of hooves told him that one of the riders was much too close. He stopped, whirled, sank to one knee, and put a slug through the man's chest. That gained him another thirty yards.

More riders joined the chase, six of them streaming from the stable in a determined pack, some riding bareback in their eagerness to catch their quarry.

Clay was surprised that he wasn't growing winded. He held to a pace that would have tired most whites and made for a solitary tree, the only haven available. Larry and the other cowboy were forty yards off but holding their fire, perhaps thinking they could wait for the rest and cut him down in a hail of lead.

Inspiration, such as it was, prompted Clay to again turn, kneel and fire. He aimed most carefully and hit Larry high on the right shoulder, the impact flipping the puncher from the saddle, limbs akimbo. The third cowboy cut loose with his rifle in retaliation, four rushed shots.

Clay suddenly grabbed at his chest, stiffened, and sprawled onto his left side, letting go of the Winchester so he could drop his hand to one of his Colts. He had to resist the temptation to take a peek as the cowpoke's horse trotted nearer and nearer.

"Did you blow out the bastard's lamp, Wade?" someone yelled from the yard.

"Sure enough did," the cowboy answered. "Ventilated the vermin right proper."

Dust tingled Clay's nose. Through slitted lids he saw hooves halt in front of him, then heard the creak of leather as Wade dismounted.

"I reckon I'll take your scalp, Injun, and show it to my folks the next time I visit home. Won't pa be plumb proud! He's never much cared for you rotten redskins."

A hand fell on Clay's shoulder and he was flipped onto his back. In a flash he drew his Colt, pressed the barrel into the cowhand's abdomen, and thumbed

133

off two shots. Wade recoiled, staggering, red spittle rimming his mouth.

Clay batted the man's rifle aside and was on the sorrel before anyone else had awakened to his ploy. Hauling on the reins, he galloped past the tree, contriving to put the trunk between him and the majority of his pursuers so their outraged volley did no harm.

Or so Clay believed until the sorrel acted up. The horse flagged and kicked with a rear leg as if trying to stomp a pesky sidewinder. Bending, Clay found a crimson trickle seeping from a hole above its knee. Any notion he had of slowing to spare the animal misery was dispelled by another series of shots from the pack on his heels.

Clay hugged the pommel and used his Winchester as an oversized quirt, repeatedly smacking the sorrel's flank to goad it on. He got to within fifty yards of the draw before the leg buckled and the horse went down. He felt it start to fall and threw himself clear. Rolling to his feet, he sprinted onward.

"Stop him!" a gruff voice bellowed. "Can't somebody stop the son of a bitch?"

Lord knows, they tried. The ground was peppered by shots, some so close they nicked Clay's buckskins and hat. He darted into the draw, all the way to the barbed wire, and slid under as the sound of pursuit rumbled off the walls and loose dirt rattled from the rims. His enemies fired as he vaulted astride the chestnut, fired as he cut and ran. A stinging sensation in his leg was a reminder he wasn't bullet-proof.

Cursing and shouting, the riders drew rein at the barbed barrier, a few shaking their fists in impotent wrath.

Clay never slowed. He'd saved his hide, but he experienced no joy. The way he saw it, he'd done poorly; he'd failed to kill the man he hated most and failed to obtain medicine that could help Delgadito. His days as the White Apache might be numbered, and without the renegades to back him up, he'd be that much easier to hunt down and kill. With every bounty hunter and soldier from Denver to Mexico City on the lookout for him, the thought was enough to almost make him wish he'd slain Gillett and gone out in a blaze of glory.

Almost, but not quite.

Chapter Ten

Delgadito, the Apache, did not expect to live much longer. His body burned with fever yet his skin felt icy cold. He had lost so much blood he was too weak to lift a finger. And overriding all was the worst pain he had ever experienced, agony so extreme it tore at the fabric of his innermost self. He expected to die and wanted to die so he would be spared further torment. And humiliation.

During his lucid moments, Delgadito felt an awful shame over having failed so many people. There had been his wife and relatives, massacred by scalp hunters because he hadn't exercised enough caution. There had been his loyal followers, warriors who had looked to him for guidance and shared his family's fate. As if that was not enough, he'd managed to turn the few survivors into outcasts shunned by their own people. And finally, he had failed himself by being unable to regain the leadership that should rightfully be his but which he had foolishly bestowed upon Lickoyee-shis-inday and apparently lost for good.

It was as if someone or something with powerful bad medicine was out to get him and had succeeded only to well, Delgadito mused.

In the Apache scheme of things, the supreme giver of life was known as *Yusn*. It was believed *Yusn* had created a number of lesser spirit beings who worked for the good of the tribe. But there were also evil spirits who took perverse delight in causing no end of misery. Apache medicine men and women were devoted to protecting their people from these harmful supernatural forces, but they weren't always successful.

Delgadito was convinced an evil *Gans,* or Mountain Spirit, intended to destroy him. Had it been possible, he would have gone to a medicine man for help. But it was too late now. He doubted he would live to see the new day dawn.

Suddenly Delgadito became aware of pressure on his brow. A hand touched lightly. Through a pale haze he saw the White Apache bending over him. Lickoyee-shis-inday spoke. In Delgadito's befuddled state the words sounded slurred, as if his ears were plugged tight with wax. He concentrated, trying to understand, a task made harder because Lickoyee-shis-inday was using English.

"—did my best, pard, but I've let you down. Don't worry none, though. Cuchillo Negro says we're bound to find some roots that will help, sooner or later."

Delgadito wanted to tell them not to bother but he couldn't move his lips. In his frustration, he groaned.

Clay thought he read confusion on the warrior's face so he switched to the Chiricahua tongue. "We are doing all we can for you, my brother. I would like to stay at this spot overnight but the *Americano soldados* are only five miles behind us and growing closer the longer we delay. Fiero is keeping watch on them in case they get too near."

Somehow Delgadito found the strength to say, "Leave me, White Apache. Take the others and go. I would like to die alone."

"A man should never give up while he can still take a breath," Clay responded, hiding his shock at the request. He'd long admired Delgadito's courage and toughness, and would never have pegged the Apache as being a quitter. "I will not desert you. I doubt the others will, either."

"Then you will waste your lives for my sake. And I am not worth it."

"You're talking nonsense," Clay said reverting to English. "Besides, it's our decision to make, not yours."

Delgadito would have liked to argue the point but a bout of paralyzing weakness silenced him. He couldn't understand why the white-eye was going to so much trouble on his behalf. But then, it had been next to impossible to understand anything Taggart did. No self-respecting Apache would allow himself to be used as Delgadito had used Lickoyee-shisinday. Chiricahuas were intelligent enough to look beyond a person's actions at the underlying motives, and only then act accordingly. Not Clay Taggart. The white-eye accepted everything at face value, as a child would do, and from what Delgadito had seen on the reservation, Taggart was typical of his kind. Sometimes Delgadito wondered if all whiteeye infants were deliberately bashed over the head shortly after birth to addle their brains.

Clay Taggart saw the deep lines of pain etching the warrior's features and gave Delgadito a friendly pat on the arm. He glanced at Cuchillo Negro, who watched their back trail, and said, "Help me with him." Then, climbing onto the chestnut, he allowed Cuchillo Negro to place Delgadito behind him and lent a hand lashing Delgadito's body to his so the warrior wouldn't fall off.

"What of Fiero?" Cuchillo Negro asked.

"He will catch up later."

"That is not what I meant. You know how he is."

"I know he can take care of himself. Right now I am more worried about Delgadito." Clay galloped eastward, reaching behind him to keep the wounded warrior from flopping about. He put Fiero from his mind entirely, confident the firebrand wouldn't do anything rash under the current circumstances.

But had Clay only known, at that very moment Fiero was pressing his rifle to his shoulder and aiming at the white-eye in buckskins who served as tracker for the cavalry patrol. His reason was simple. He figured if he killed the tracker, the troopers would be unable to find White Apache and the others.

Fiero lay under mesquite on a knoll seventy yards from the soldiers. He had already picked out not only the scout but the *Americano* in charge and the bearded bellower who always relayed the officer's orders to the men.

During Fiero's short stay on the reservation, he had made it his business to study the various Army patrols he'd seen and to learn all he could about how they were organized. He'd learned that men who wore large patches on their shoulders were called officers and were the ones in charge, while those who wore colorful stripes on their sleeves were known as sergeants and although these sergeants served under the officers they had as much, if not more, influence with the troopers.

So Fiero easily identified the officer leading the patrol, and he knew the bellower was the sergeant. He observed them conferring with the tracker, who then forked a saddle and rode slowly forward. The man was skilled, but not as skilled as an Apache. Were the situation reversed, Fiero would practically fly along the trail.

The firebrand settled the front sight on the scout's sternum and aligned the rear sight with the front. Fiero allowed the scout to ride another twenty yards before he squeezed the trigger. The officer gaped in surprise when the scout hit the ground but recovered to shout commands and set the whole patrol into motion, bearing down on the knoll.

Scrambling backwards, Fiero dashed to his bay and leaped on its back. Legs flapping, he galloped southward, not eastward as his friends had gone. He intended to lead the patrol on a merry chase and slake his thirst for battle in the bargain.

Holding formation, four abreast, the soldiers swept over the rise and spotted Fiero. He looked back and grinned, mocking them. To fool the troopers into thinking they were gaining he held the bay in, and when they began to narrow the gap he let the bay have its head and pulled ahead.

Fiero had been pursued by soldiers before. Each time there had been a pattern to the chase. Invariably, the *Americanos* rode fast and hard initially, but when they saw they couldn't prevail, they gave up. Always it was the same, a fact Fiero could exploit to his advantage.

For over a mile the soldiers doggedly ate Fiero's dust, until at a barked order from the officer they slowed to a walk. Fiero kept on riding at full gallop until he was out of their sight, then he swung to the west in a wide loop that brought him up on the patrol without them knowing. Tying the bay, he stalked through the brush and shortly located the troopers taking their leisure while their winded mounts rested.

Fiero wormed his way within rifle range. He studied the uniforms and located both the young officer and the sergeant. Propping both elbows, he aimed at the bellower, going for a head shot. The sergeant was yelling at a pair of soldiers, who took the outburst without complaint. Yet another white trait Fiero sneered at. For any man to tolerate such abuse was unthinkable.

Once more the sergeant consulted the officer. Then the bearded man removed his hat to wipe his brow and gaze at the sun as if gauging the amount of daylight left.

Fiero was ready. He fired, and instantly backpedaled, annoyed that at the very moment he'd shot, the sergeant had stooped to tug at a boot. Every last soldier scurried for cover, including the lucky sergeant and the officer.

Speeding to the bay, Fiero rode northward, his expert eye choosing the thickest growth, the most difficult terrain. He had little doubt the soldiers would be hopelessly inept in tracking him without the scout, and an hour later when he had circled again he saw them strung out in a ragged line seeking sign.

Fiero laid on his belly in high weeds and pinpointed the officer, but not the sergeant. He counted the patrol, learned there were four men missing, and guessed the sergeant was out looking for him.

Fiero settled for the officer, who squatted beside a flat rock on which a big piece of paper had been spread out. The officer and another man were running their fingers over the paper, then pointing in different directions. Maps, such papers were called. Fiero couldn't understand why the white-eyes relied on them. Apaches were taught to memorize the countryside through which they passed and to make note of prominent landmarks for future reference. If someone were to blindfold him and take him anywhere within a hundred and fifty mile radius, he would find his way back again with unerring accuracy.

The officer stood and stretched. Fiero sighted on the man's face and fired. Sent reeling by the impact, the officer fell among his men. Panic seized the troopers as they scooped up their carbines, went prone, and started firing at anything and everything.

Fiero stayed put to see if they would charge him. Amazingly, none had any idea where he was. They wasted scores of bullets before a skinny man with two stripes on his sleeves restored order. It wasn't long afterward that the sergeant and the other missing men arrived.

Slaying a few more would have been child's play, but Fiero did not. He studied them, learning how they reacted, learning their weaknesses for future encounters. Knowing an enemy was essential. Had the Chiricahuas known more about the white-eyes, they might have held out much longer than they did.

The soldiers were mounting. Fiero saw them form into four groups, one facing east, another west, the others north and south. He wondered what they were up to, and the answer came when the sergeant bellowed and they exploded across the plain, spreading out as they did, forming into a giant ring that kept expanding the farther they rode.

Startled by the brilliant strategy, Fiero ran to the bay. He had wasted so much time that several of the white-eyes were almost on him. They shouted excitedly as he bore to the northeast. Sporadic carbine fire sped him along. He wasn't worried in the least because he counted on the soldiers giving up after a while, as they always did. But these troopers proved to be the exception to the rule.

Those with poor horses fell out of the chase first. Others lasted a few miles more. Approximately eight or nine were on superior animals, and they stuck to Fiero like sap to a tree. He plunged into thorny brush but they were undeterred. He wound along a narrow gully for over two miles, thinking their poor horsemanship would be their undoing, but they showed they were as good as he was and actually gained ground.

The bay was slick with sweat when Fiero broke into open country and flew due north. The horse would last another ten miles, he judged, but by then he hoped to be in chaparral where he could elude the *Americanos* on foot.

A grim smile lit Fiero's countenance. He lived for warfare, as had his father, and his father's father. That his life was in danger added zest to his existence, not detracted from it. Killing without being killed was the Apache creed, and it was a way of life in which Fiero passionately believed. He would never accept boring reservation life as had the tame Chiricahuas; he would rather be flayed alive.

Although not given to introspection, Fiero had often pondered on the fate of his people. He had been hurt beyond measure when so many succumbed to the white invaders after offering token resistance. Fiero had argued with the leaders who advocated surrender until he was hoarse, without result. They had wanted peace at any cost, even at the price of their freedom, their integrity.

Fiero had seen the terrible toll the war took on his people, but he had been adamant. No one had the right to steal their ancestral land. No one had the right to tell them how they should live, how they should dress and act. The whites had gone so far as to require warriors to cut their long hair short as a symbol of their peaceful intentions, a symbol Fiero regarded as a mark of cowardice, as the final degrading act in a long line of requirements that had stripped the Chiricahua warriors of their manhood and reduced them to little better than well dressed dogs fit only to grovel at the feet of their white masters.

To Fiero it was unimportant that many of the white soldiers held no personal enmity toward his people. It was unimportant that many serving in Arizona would rather be elsewhere. They had taken his land, enslaved his people, and they would pay dearly for their audacity.

Presently Fiero reached the chaparral. He slanted to the right, then to the left. When the soldiers were temporarily blocked from view, he prodded the bay to go faster, then coiled his legs up under him, looked for a break in the brush, and leaped. He hit the ground running and was on his stomach before the dust of the bay's passage had settled.

His animal continued on at breakneck speed. The troopers poured around a bush, saw it, and never slowed, streaking past Fiero in a thundering string. Rising, he stared at their backs until they were gone. Tricking white-eyes was no challenge, he reflected.

"*Tu no vale nada,*" Fiero said aloud to himself, and turned to head southward.

Twenty yards away stood a trooper with a leveled carbine, the reins of his horse held loosely in one hand. The animal was fidgeting and limped badly.

144

Fiero had his own Winchester in the crook of his left arm. He made no move to use it since to do so invited certain death. The soldier addressed him but Fiero had no idea what the white-eye said. When the trooper motioned, he gathered that he was to put down his rifle, and slowly. The *Americano* seemed to relax a bit after he did.

Fiero had to do something. Soon the others would catch the bay and promptly swing around to search for him. He had a knife on the back of his right hip but drawing it would be too obvious.

The trooper motioned again, signaling for Fiero to step closer. Fiero did, and was made to understand he should kneel. Evidently pleased, the soldier tipped his carbine skyward and banged off two rapid shots.

Fiero's fingers were inches from his knife. He pretended to be cowed and bowed his head while secretly easing his hand to the hilt. The *Americano* let go of his mount's reins and edged to the left, the carbine trained on Fiero's head.

Fiero froze to deceive the white-eye into thinking he was going to submit without a fight, but he watched closely out of the corner of his eye. When the trooper twisted to scan the brush for his companions, Fiero whipped out the hunting knife and threw it in an underhand toss he had perfected through long practice.

The cavalryman had sensed something was amiss and turned as the warrior sprang into action, with the result that the long steel blade bit into the base of his throat before he could snap off a shot. Horrified, he clutched at the knife but couldn't get a grip on the slippery weapon.

Fiero grabbed the man's fallen carbine by the barrel and swung it in a vicious arc that caught the trooper flush on the face and felled him where he stood. Tossing the carbine aside, Fiero reclaimed his Winchester and his knife, then climbed on the soldier's mount. He didn't care if it had gone lame or not. He had to get out of there before more white-eyes arrived.

Wheeling eastward, Fiero goaded the reluctant horse into the chaparral, pausing once to break off a limb. The animal limped badly and grew worse as time went on. Whenever it slowed, Fiero lashed it with the limb so fiercely the blows drew blood and left nasty welts. The horse would then pick up the pace.

While Fiero's actions would have appalled a typical Easterner, he was unfazed. To Apaches, horses were just so much brute flesh, to be used as the Apaches saw fit. And since most animals wound up in cooking pots, seldom did a warrior allow himself to become attached to one.

In this instance, Fiero fully intended to ride the cavalry mount into the ground in order to put as much distance behind him as he could. He lashed and kicked and slapped, going well over five miles before the horse reached the end of its rope. On the slope of a small hill it finally faltered and would not go on no matter what he did. Leaping down, Fiero slit its throat and left it thrashing in a spreading pool of blood to die a slow but relatively painless death.

Legs pumping, Fiero scaled the hill, stopping at the top to check on the *Americanos*. They were still after him, all right, about two miles back. He jogged on, his pantherish muscles rippling, his stocky form flowing over the ground with exceptional, surprising grace.

Fiero ran for several miles, showing no signs of fatigue when he eventually halted at the edge of a narrow gully. It was so narrow that he could leap to the other side, yet it was thirty feet deep. On seeing it, he grinned, and when Fiero grinned, someone was bound to suffer.

Chopping off enough vegetation to cover the top took a quarter of an hour. Next Fiero pulled out entire bushes by their roots and arranged them so that they formed a seemingly natural aisle leading to the brink of the gully. Retracing his steps to a point fifty yards away, he snapped off a branch in so obvious a spot that even the white-eyes couldn't miss it. Then he crossed to the other side and hid.

The *soldados* were not long in coming. Seven of them, riding warily, the sergeant in the lead. He was the one who spotted the broken branch and called out to his fellows. In a compact group they thundered along the fake aisle, and because of Fiero's cleverly arranged bushes they were ignorant of the gully's existence until the sergeant's horse pitched into it with a panicked whinny. Two others suffered the same fate before the rest collected their wits and reined up.

Fiero thought their antics laughable. The three mounts that had fallen into the gully were neighing in an anguished chorus. The soldiers themselves were cursing and shouting to one another. He saw a grizzled one take a rope and lower it down. In turn, each of those who had taken a spill were hoisted out. None appeared the worse for wear except the sergeant, who held his left arm much like a bird would hold a crippled wing.

The troopers talked in low tones while staring down into the gully. Four of them formed a line, aimed their carbines, and blasted away until the last strangled whinny died to a gurgling wheeze. Riding double, the crestfallen *Americanos* headed back.

147

Fiero stood when they were gone. He walked to the gully, surveyed the carnage he had wrought, and quickly clambered over the edge. He picked a fine black and cut off a sizeable piece of its haunch.

Climbing out was simple. The warrior gathered enough kindling and wood and soon had a small fire crackling in a concealed nook. He trimmed the hide from his steak, impaled the dripping meat on a stick, and hunkered down to await his meal.

It gave Fiero pleasure to review his clash with the white-eyes and to think of the wailing women who would lament the loss of their loved ones. Countless Apache women had done the same in recent times, as one by one the proud Apache men were wiped out by the locusts from the north.

Fiero remembered how, many winters ago, he had heard white trappers boast that there were more of their kind than there were blades of grass on the prairie. Naturally, Fiero had believed the trappers to be rank braggarts who couldn't hold their whiskey. But the men had been right, after all, and the Chiricahuas had paid dearly for resisting the white invasion.

Numbers and firepower. Those were the keys to the white victory. Fiero was convinced that the war would have ended differently if the two sides had been evenly matched. Pueblos, Spaniards, Mexicans—the Apaches had beaten them all. It had taken a well-armed, limitless horde to do that which no one else had been able to do—subjugate the Apaches.

A soft rustling drew Fiero's gaze to a slithering rattler. He had the horse meat, but he darted over anyway and sank his blade into the snake's head as it curled to strike. A single, powerful stroke severed the tail, which he stuck in his breechcloth as he returned to the fire. He would save it, and later, when he had occasion to steal horses, the rattles would come in handy.

Fiero stared at the eastern horizon. By now, he mused, the others were halfway to their sanctuary. Being afoot, he'd take days to catch up. Not that it upset him. He preferred to raid alone, to kill alone, to exalt in the prowess that made him what he was; namely, one of the last true Apaches. Like Delgadito, Cuchillo Negro, and Ponce. And, yes, to a lesser degree, much like the White Apache.

Chapter Eleven

They were high in the mountains, less than a mile from Sweet Grass, when Cuchillo Negro reined up and announced, "I must go look for him."

Clay Taggart halted. "Do what you have to," he said. "I can manage by myself from here."

"I know he is a grown man and can look out for himself," Cuchillo Negro justified his decision, "but there are so few of us left, and he has a talent for getting into trouble. His hot head makes him commit acts that wiser warriors would know not to do."

"There is no need to explain."

The warrior lifted his reins, then said, "I would be grateful if you did not tell him I was concerned. He would think me weak."

"My ears never heard your words," Clay said, touching the upcurled brim of his hat. He rode on, anxious to reach their hideout so Delgadito would at last enjoy a long spell of rest and recuperation. It amazed him that the warrior still lived. Several times Delgadito had teetered on the edge of eternity, and in each instance the Apache had rallied, tapping an inner reservoir of endurance for which his tribe was widely noted.

A hawk circling high in the azure sky vented a shrill shriek as it winged lower after prey. Clay watched the streaking predator swoop onto a rocky slope and heard the death squeal of the animal it slew. Not until he came to live among the renegades had he fully realized how harsh a mistress Nature could be. In the wild, the only law was the survival of the fittest, a law that applied to beasts and man alike.

The Apaches had lived by this law for ages. In the unforgiving crucible of tooth and claw they had learned to meet Nature on its own terms, and endure. It had forged them into the fearless fighters they were. Or rather, the fighters they had been before their spirit was broken by the U.S. Army. By the whites. By his kind.

The thought bothered Clay. Of late he'd developed the habit of regarding himself as more Apache than white. Like a boiling kettle about to bubble over, he simmered with conflicting loyalties. On the one hand, part of him couldn't abide the cruel conduct of renegades who wiped out innocent families. On the other, he now saw the state of affairs through Apache eyes and had to admit their outrage was understandable. Who should he side with, he wondered? His own kind? When they had stolen his ranch out from under him and tried to make him do a cottonwood jig? He owed them nothing. Not a solitary mother's son of them. Let them all rot in hell.

151

The Apaches he owed a great deal. They'd saved his life, doctored him, fed and clothed him, accepted him as one of their own. They'd pulled his fat out of the fire when he was taken prisoner by an army patrol. And they'd stood by him when some of their own kind wanted to kill him. In short, the members of Delgadito's small band had done the sort of things true pards did for one another. So maybe, he mused, it was time for him to stop thinking of ever going back to his old life. Maybe he should throw his lot in with the Chiricahuas for keeps, come what may.

To enter Sweet Grass, a rider had to negotiate a long, winding ravine so high sunlight seldom bathed the bottom. Clay became absorbed in the many twists and turns, his left hand behind his back to hold Delgadito in place. He studied the ground to see if anyone had been through since they left and saw only the tracks made recently by the string Ponce had brought back.

Presently the ravine widened and the hidden valley unfolded before him. Clay sought evidence of a fire but saw none. Angling toward the cliff, he stayed vigilant, remembering the attack by Nah-kah-yen. He didn't think the Army would be loco enough to send in another scout so soon after losing one of their best, but he'd learned the hard way never to take anything for granted.

Oddly, there was no trace of Ponce at the camp. Figuring the youth was off hunting, Clay made Delgadito comfortable, then let the chestnut loose to graze. He took a water bag to the stream to fill it, and as he neared the pool where he had bathed last, he drew up short on beholding a tall pole imbedded in the soft soil at the water's edge. It wasn't the pole that startled him; it was the grisly head someone had impaled on top. Stunned, Clay advanced slowly, noting the long dark hair and butchered features of an Indian woman. An Apache, he deduced, a young maiden, going by the smoothness of her skin and her tresses, which although matted with blood and dirt had not yet lost all of their former luxuriant sheen.

The implications hit Clay like a bolt of lightning and he promptly squatted and brought the Winchester to bear. Ponce's absence took on a whole new meaning. He almost called out the warrior's name but caught himself in time.

Setting the water skin down, Clay sidled to the pole. There were tracks, a single set, so faint they gave the illusion the man lacked corporal substance. Clay knew better. Some Apaches were so light on their feet their prints were hard to read, just like these.

The killer had gone toward the stream, so Clay did likewise. He estimated the pole had been put in place ten to twelve hours earlier, so it was likely the man responsible was long gone.

The significance of the ghastly trophy eluded Clay. Was it meant as a threat of some sort? Or was it an Apache hex, tied in somehow with their belief in bad medicine and evil powers?

The tracks led into the water. Clay walked a few dozen feet in both directions, seeking the point where the killer emerged. On the opposite bank on the right were crushed blades of grass. He forded to examine them but was disappointed to learn a deer had been responsible.

Clay didn't know what to do next. It wouldn't do much good to aimlessly traipse around the valley looking for sign. He should make the killer come to him, provided the man was still in Sweet Grass.

First he must find a safe spot to secret Delgadito.

The thought electrified Clay into plunging across the stream and racing to the cliff. He had to skirt some pines before he saw the site clearly, and his pulse quickened when he discovered Delgadito gone. The killer had snuck in and toted the warrior off! He scoured the terrain in rising alarm but saw nothing other than the horses.

Kneeling, Clay found the same set of prints as those at the stream, only deeper because the killer had thrown Delgadito over one shoulder. Swiftly, Clay went in pursuit. The trail led along the base of the cliff for a hundred yards, then moved to the left, to the bottom of a slope covered with timber.

From behind a tree trunk Clay did as Delgadito had taught him and scrutinized every pine, every weed clump, every blade of grass. The trick lay in detecting where the pattern had been broken. Living things weren't ghosts. They couldn't pass through the wilderness without leaving some evidence of their passage. But this one had.

Clay continued his search, realizing his enemy was highly skilled. Rising, he ran to the left to use a thicket as cover as he ascended, but he had no more than gone three strides when a huge mallet seemed to slam into his torso and he was catapulted through the air. He glimpsed the earth rushing up to meet him, then the breath was jarred from his lungs.

Dazed, certain he had been shot, Clay rolled onto his stomach and crawled to a log. Gradually he recovered. His life had been spared by the merest fluke, the bullet having hit his rifle, striking the side plate and ricocheting into the stock. Both had been shattered, but better them than his rib cage.

Quick Killer

Placing the useless Winchester down, Clay drew a Colt, then crept to the end of the downed tree and peeked around the twisted roots. Whoever shot at him must know where he was hiding. He needed to get out of there before the bushwhacker changed position and picked him off. Cocking the pistol, he dug his toes into the soil and bunched his legs.

"Maybe you make this easy on both of us, eh, Lickoyee-shis-inday?"

The unexpected hail rooted Clay in place.

"I know you still live, white man. I shot at your rifle on purpose. Throw out your other guns and I give you my word I not kill you."

"Who are you?" Clay wanted to know.

"Tats-ah-das-ay-go."

"Quick Killer?" Clay translated.

"You have heard of me," the man said, pride and arrogance equally thick in his tone.

"Can't say as I have."

A pause ensued. Clay stared at the nearest trees, ten feet off, and debated whether to make a try for them. He didn't care to squat there like a sitting duck when his foe was probably on the move.

Unknown to him, he was right. Quick Killer was thirty yards to the northwest, running to a boulder. Ducking down, he cupped a hand to his mouth and shouted, "But I have heard of you, White Apache. The Army wants you very bad. There is much money on your head, dead or alive."

"And you aim to collect," Clay responded, inching forward. He wanted to keep the man talking, to distract him long enough to reach the timber.

"I do," Quick Killer admitted. He was feeling quite sure of himself. Very shortly, all his careful planning, all his diligent effort, would pay off handsomely and he would not let anything go wrong.

"It won't be easy," Clay vowed. He was ready to make his dash, but he'd rather know where the killer was hiding first. To that end, he had to keep the man talking. "Others have tried and wound up worm food."

"I am better than them, Taggart," Quick Killer boasted. "I am the best."

"Why bother taking me alive?" Clay asked, probing the vegetation.

Quick Killer didn't answer right away. Initially, he'd intended to take White Apache in dead, but after thinking about it some more, he'd realized that practically anyone lucky enough to be in the right place at the right time could put a bullet through Taggart's brain. Taking White Apache back in one piece would be a greater challenge and would add more luster to Quick Killer's reputation.

"Did you hear me?" Clay goaded, deciding not to wait any longer.

"I hear," Quick Killer said.

And Clay was off like a jackrabbit, bounding into the pines and diving flat. He chose a wide trunk to lie behind and surveyed the slope above, wondering if the one who called himself Quick Killer had seen his move.

Indeed, the scout had. Quick Killer grinned and slid to the left a dozen feet. Propping his rifle on an earthen hump, he scanned the trees below and spied the lower half of a leg in plain sight. Snuggling his cheek to the Winchester, he sighted on White Apache's ankle. His finger caressed the cool trigger in anticipation. Then he heard footsteps.

Twisting, the scout surveyed the woods above. He listened to a rustling noise and a loud snap, as of a twig breaking underfoot. For a moment he thought someone was sneaking up on him but the sounds

156

faded away as the person did the same. Since there was only one man it could be, Quick Killer leaped to his feet and sprinted higher.

Clay Taggart raised his Colt. He only had a glimpse of buckskins and a red headband but he banged off two rapid shots anyway, neither of which appeared to have any effect. He couldn't understand why Quick Killer was running off. Not one to look a gift horse in the mouth, he pushed upright and dashed madly toward the cliff.

Once there, Clay went into thick brush bordering the bottom and ran for over sixty yards. Here the cliff ended and a steep incline brought him slowly but surely to the summit. He had to stop often to seek solid purchase, and at one point he leaned out to see if the killer had followed him. He leaned much too far, losing his balance and nearly plummeting to the bottom.

At the summit Clay moved well back from the edge so he couldn't be seen from below and hastened to a vantage point directly above the camp. A Colt in both hands, he scoured the ponderosas but couldn't find Tats-ah-das-ay-go.

Quick Killer was in dense growth, close to a clearing where he had left Delgadito. Too cautious to blunder into the open, he circled the clearing, annoyed to see it empty. Delgadito's tracks were on the far side, leading higher, the footprints revealing Delgadito had moved with a short, shuffling stride, as befitted a man on his last legs. It would be no time at all before Quick Killer recaptured him.

The scout climbed to a ridge and hurried down the other side. He knew how weak Delgadito had been and counted on soon finding the unconscious warrior. Yet he went as far as an arrow could fly and did not come on the renegade. He would have gone farther but the tracks abruptly ended.

Mystified, Quick Killer searched in an ever widening circle, his movements growing more urgent as it became clear Delgadito had apparently vanished without leaving a clue to how it had been done. Quick Killer had never lost a trail before, and to do so now, at the worst of times, was doubly vexing.

Going to the last set of tracks, Quick Killer studied the partial impressions and the grass around them. He reasoned that Delgadito had tricked him and all he had to do was ascertain how. But it proved more difficult than he would have imagined.

Quick Killer chafed at the delay. He imagined White Apache catching a horse at that very moment, and foresaw the white-eye bringing the rest of the band back. Now that he'd lost the element of surprise, he'd either have to flee Sweet Grass before the renegades got there or resort to the special ploy he had in mind. And running from a fight wasn't in his nature. Giving the area one last survey, Quick Killer jogged off.

If the scout had looked back, he would have seen a low limb on one of the trees move and a face seared by affliction and anger appear. But Quick Killer was in a rush, and he didn't slow until he reached the top of the ridge and was starting down the other side. A glint of sunlight off metal caught his eye, sparkling briefly on top of a cliff to the southeast.

Quick Killer ducked into a cluster of aspens. The interplay of sunlight and shadows from passing clouds that dappled the cliff kept him from seeing the prone figure until it moved. "White Apache," Quick Killer said aloud softly, admiring his foe's mettle. Few adversaries were so resourceful.

Cutting deeper into the aspens, Quick Killer headed for the slope flanking the cliff. He no longer needed to rely on his special ploy. White Apache had unwittingly played right into his hands.

Over on the cliff, Clay fidgeted with impatience. He knew he shouldn't but couldn't help himself. The longer it took him to take care of Quick Killer, the less likely Delgadito would be alive when it was over. He snaked to his right a few yards, then crawled to the left. Neither in the valley proper or on any of the slopes was there any movement.

Clay glanced toward the entrance to Sweet Grass, wishing Cuchillo Negro and Fiero would show. The three of them would make short shrift of the man in buckskins. But he had no idea when they would arrive. It might be minutes, hours, or days. Something told him whenever it was, they would be too late.

As Clay fretted, Tats-ah-das-ay-go stalked steadily closer up the sparsely treed slope on the back side of the cliff. There were enough boulders and shallow depressions to serve his purpose, but he had to climb much too slowly to suit him. Near the top he had to adopt a virtual turtle's pace, resorting to all the stealth of which he was capable. Once he captured the White Apache, he would hunt down Delgadito and be on his way. The other renegades were unimportant, no more than mad dogs who would amount to nothing without Delgadito's leadership.

Up on the craggy heights, Clay Taggart concluded he had wasted his time. Quick Killer wasn't coming after him. Sliding back from the rim, he pushed to his knees and shoved the Colts into their holsters. He'd go down the back slope and swing around to outflank the killer. With a little luck, it would all be over by sunset. Standing, Clay backed away from the cliff, watching to be sure Tats-ah-das-ay-go didn't appear below.

Quick Killer couldn't believe his eyes. The white fool was backing straight toward him. He rose and raised his rifle on high, the stock poised to bash White Apache on the head. Three more steps and he would have his prisoner.

Clay took the first step, his palms resting on the butts of his pistols. He'd like to get his hands on another rifle, and he knew where the renegades had a cache of plunder that included several Winchesters, a couple of Henrys, and a few old Sharps. Before tangling with Quick Killer, he'd fetch one.

The scout saw White Apache start to turn. Smirking wickedly, Tats-ah-das-ay-go brought the heavy stock sweeping down.

Chapter Twelve

During the many weeks Delgadito had spent teaching Clay Taggart Apache ways, the renegade had complained several times that Clay was as ungainly as a drunken mule. "You must have eyes in feet, Lickoyee-shis-inday," the warrior cautioned over and over in his imperfect English. "Many rocks, many holes. You trip over every one."

"I ain't doing that poorly, pard," Clay had countered, knowing full well his friend was right.

With practice, Clay had improved. But not enough to keep him from occasionally making mistakes that caused the warriors to look at him as if he were a blundering five year old.

This would have been one of those times. For as Clay turned without looking, his left foot came down on a rock. It wasn't big or jagged but it was smooth and his foot slipped out from under him just as a solid object flashed past his face. He fell to one knee and looked up into the feral features of Quick Killer.

The scout swung again, driving the stock low, but Clay was able to throw himself to the side. In a lightning draw Clay's Colt cleared leather, yet as fast as he was, Quick Killer was faster. A moccasin flicked out, connecting with Clay's wrist, and the nickel-plated Colt went flying.

Quick Killer tried to brain Clay a third time. Clay jerked backward, grabbed the rifle and pulled, jerking Quick Killer off his feet.

Clay tried to flip out from under, but Tats-ah-das-ay-go fell on top of him. Each had a hold on the Winchester. Grappling mightily, they surged this way and that, neither gaining the upper hand. Quick Killer broke the deadlock by ramming his foot into Clay's gut while simultaneously letting go.

Clay was sent rolling. He cast the Winchester from him and dropped his left hand to his second Colt, thinking he could draw and shoot much quicker than he could level the rifle and work the lever. And he was right, to a point. The Colt was arcing up when Quick Killer pounced.

Iron fingers clamped on Clay's windpipe, choking off his air. He saw a glittering knife spear at his shoulder and narrowly evaded it. To save himself he had to drop the Colt and seize Quick Killer's wrist so he could hold the knife at bay.

Tats-ah-das-ay-go had changed his mind. He no longer cared to take White Apache alive, not when his life was at stake. A dead body would be better than no body at all. So he strove his utmost to sink his blade into the white-eye's heart while choking the life from the American.

Clay exerted all his strength, yet couldn't pry the fingers from his throat. Meanwhile, Quick Killer's blade dipped closer and closer to his shirt. In another few moments either the knife would drink deep of his blood or his lungs would burst from lack of air. Desperation drove him to employ a weapon he rarely did; his teeth.

By suddenly shifting his weight, Clay was able to yank Quick Killer's wrist close to his mouth. He bit hard, his teeth sheering through skin and flesh. The salty tang of warm blood filled his mouth.

Quick Killer's eyes widened and his mouth parted in a soundless cry. Frantic, he tried to tear his wrist free and only succeeded in making the wound worse as Taggart's teeth ripped off a big chunk of flesh. To save his wrist he released the white-eye's neck and planted a fist in his foe's stomach.

Clay Taggart relaxed his jaws and heaved. Gagging for breath, he got to his feet and looked about for his six-shooters. He saw one and tried to snatch it but Quick Killer darted in front of him and made a vicious swipe with that big knife. Clay retreated, barely staying one step ahead of his enraged enemy.

Blood poured from Tats-ah-das-ay-go's wrist and a tingling sensation was creeping up his arm. He executed a wide slash, then adroitly tossed his knife from one hand to the other so his good arm was employed. Continuing to swing, he nicked Taggart's shoulder.

Clay saw the Winchester out of the corner of an eye. He tried darting over to it but Quick Killer guessed his intent and dashed in front of him. Defenseless, Clay was forced to back up as Tats-ah-das-ay-go rained blow after blow at him.

Neither of them paid any attention to their surroundings. The first intimation Clay had of a new danger came when he ducked under a cut and skipped to the rear, only to have his left foot cleave thin air. Shifting, he saw the precipice inches from his other foot and realized how close he had come to meeting his Maker. He faced front, expecting Quick Killer to press him harder. Strangely, the man just stood there.

"You have nowhere left to go," Tats-ah-das-ay-go said, pleased at the accidental outcome. Now he had a chance to take White Apache back alive, provided the white-eye listened to reason. "Give up and I let you live."

"Go to hell!" Clay responded, tensed to move either way depending on how Quick Killer attacked.

"Most men not so eager to die," Tats-ah-das-ay-go noted. While he would never admit as much, secretly he admired Taggart's fighting spirit. Not one of the many renegades he had tracked down over the years had proven half so difficult to subdue.

"Most men don't have bounty on their heads," Clay snapped, surprised Quick Killer was content to talk instead of finishing him off. "You'll have to earn your money the hard way, bounty hunter."

"I no bounty hunter. I am scout."

"Scouts wear uniforms," Clay pointed out, suspecting the man had lied.

"All but Tats-ah-das-ay-go. I do as I please."

"Were you sent after Delgadito or me, or both?" Clay asked, his future hinging on the answer. He'd about had his fill of his own kind. They'd cheated him, stolen from him, tried to rub him out. The marshal of Tombstone had the long arm of civilian authority arrayed against him. And now the government itself must be intent on doing him wrong. It was the last straw, if true. "Which?" he prompted.

Quick Killer

Quick Killer wasn't about to confess that he'd decided to hunt the band on his own, without official approval. He thought that if he lied, it would anger White Apache, perhaps even make Taggart mad enough to want to go back and confront those responsible, thereby rendering his job a lot easier. "They send me after you," he said. "Tell me to bring you. Say take as many moons as I want."

"I figured as much," Clay growled.

"So you come back, eh?" Quick Killer prodded. "You have your say. Tell army what you think."

"Never."

"You fool, white man."

Clay bristled, clenching his fists so tight his knuckles paled. "Don't call me that! No one is ever to call me that again. From here on out, for better or for worse, I'm the White Apache."

"You think you are Indian?" Quick Killer scoffed. "Take lifetime of living to be Apache."

"Just for the trimmings, I reckon."

"I do not understand."

"The trimmings," Clay repeated, moving a few inches to the right. He wanted to keep the scout jawing a little while longer, long enough for him to reach a small mound of loose earth a yard away. "Speaking the tongue fluently and knowing all the customs and such are what I call the trimmings of being an Apache. But there's a hell of a lot more to it than that."

"Oh?" Quick Killer grinned, amused by the notion of a white man claiming kinship with his father's people.

"Being an Apache has to do with what's in here," Clay said, thumping his chest over his heart and taking another short sideways step. "It has to do with craving freedom more than anything else, and not letting other folks tell you how you should live."

"You are wrong, white-eye," Quick Killer said. "Being Apache is in blood, not in heart. And you have wrong kind of blood."

"Which one of us is the renegade and which one is working for the white sons of bitches who make a habit out of stealing other folks' land?"

"You dare say you are more Indian than me?" Quick Killer rejoined in disbelief. "My father and all his fathers were Indians. Yours were white."

"Maybe so, but I don't want anything to do with the white part of me from now on. Like I told you, I'm Lickoyee-shis-inday."

"You are loco."

Clay had edged close enough to make his play, but there was one thing he needed to know beforehand. "Delgadito didn't think so." He paused. "Speaking of which, what did you do with him, you murdering bastard?"

The fiery insult scorched Quick Killer's pride but he controlled his temper. "Delgadito is alive," he said, "until I am done with you. Then he dies."

"You're counting your chickens before they're hatched, *hombre*," Clay taunted.

"We will see," Tats-ah-das-ay-go said, and lunged, extending his arm to its fullest in order to pierce the white man's torso.

Clay was in motion before the thrust commenced. He dipped, scooped up a handful of the dirt, and flung it squarely into the half-breed's eyes.

Quick Killer was a shade too slow in reacting. He saw the *Americano* bend but didn't divine Taggart's intent until the dirt was in flight. He shut his eyes, too late to keep some of the dirt from getting in and setting them to watering fiercely. Back-pedaling, he blinked over and over and wiped at them with his free hand, all the time swinging his knife in a random pattern to keep his quarry at bay.

There had been a time when the tactic would have worked, a time before Clay Taggart came to live among the Chiricahua renegades, before he learned to wield a knife as expertly as he already did a six-shooter. He'd learned well, this White Apache, and he resorted to his knowledge now as he glided to the right, crouched low to the ground and sprang, tackling Quick Killer around the ankles.

Quick Killer felt himself falling and stabbed at where he thought Taggart would be. But White Apache had let go and moved beyond reach. As the knife arm descended, White Apache pounced, gripping Quick Killer's wrist even as he drove his shoulder up and under Quick Killer's arm. Bending, White Apache heaved, throwing all his weight into the act.

Quick Killer felt air brush his cheeks and braced for the impact sure to follow. A second went by. Two. Three. And still he had not hit the ground. Furiously brushing at his eyes, he wondered how high the white-eye had thrown him. Abruptly, his vision cleared, and he realized it wasn't how high that mattered, it was how far.

Stark fear such as Quick Killer had never known seized him as he gaped up at the receding rim of the cliff and the grim avenger staring down at him. "Noooooo!" he howled. "It cannot end like this!"

White Apache's lips formed a mocking smile.

Thrashing and kicking, Quick Killer went into a frenzied panic. He twisted, saw the cliff face sweeping past him just feet away. Thoughtlessly, he reached out and tried grabbing hold to arrest his fall. His fingertips scraped solid rock, the rough surface shearing the skin from his fingers like a hot knife searing butter. He cried out, glanced down, and his stomach seemed to leap into his throat. He couldn't breathe, couldn't think. This wasn't supposed to happen, he told himself. He was Tats-ah-das-ay-go, the most feared of Army scouts, the man who had brought in more renegades than anyone else. His medicine was powerful, the most powerful of all. He couldn't be beaten by a deluded white-eye who wasn't half as skillful.

The ground loomed steadily closer, steadily larger, becoming Quick Killer's whole universe. The wind plucked at his buckskins, at his hair. He wanted to scream his defiance, to die as he had lived, but his insides had turned to water and were trickling down his leg.

The White Apache stood gazing down at the crimson smear of pulped flesh and busted bones for some time. Then he reclaimed his Colts and the scout's rifle and hastened to the base of the cliff. He was en route to the slope where Quick Killer had shot at him when a weaving figure stumbled into the open and called his name.

White Apache reached Delgadito as the warrior's legs buckled. He picked up the Chiricahua, carried him to the camp, and covered him with blankets. After building a fire, he went for water and permitted Delgadito to drink his fill. "How do you feel?" he asked in Apache.

"Much better. The fever has left me."

A hand to the brow confirmed it. White Apache nodded and said in English, "I always knew you were a tough son of a gun, pard."

For the first time since Delgadito met Clay Taggart, he didn't mind being called that. "I owe you my life. Again."

"I cannot claim all the credit. Cuchillo Negro and Fiero helped."

"What of Ponce?"

White Apache started, then blurted, "I plumb forgot about him. You lie still while I have a look-see." Since he hadn't seen Quick Killer's mount from the cliff, he figured it must be hidden among the trees. Twenty minutes of thorough searching brought him to a clearing in which two horses were ground hitched. On one, gagged and tied hand and foot with his legs lashed together under the animal's belly, sat Ponce.

"I thought you would be dead," White Apache said as he tugged the gag out.

"The breed was going to use me as a decoy," Ponce said. "He bragged how he would slap my horse and send it running past all of you and counted on you shooting me by mistake." The young warrior smoldered with wrath. "Where is the dog that I might kill him?"

"Dead."

"Who? You?"

"He tried to fly and forgot to coat himself with feathers first."

"You speak in riddles. Men are not birds."

"So he found out."

Two days later Cuchillo Negro and Fiero arrived at Sweet Grass. They were delighted to find Delgadito recovering, indignant to hear of Tats-ah-das-ay-go's attempt to destroy their band, and upset to learn that Lickoyee-shis-inday had left the day before on a special errand. To all their questions, Delgadito would only say that, "He took a gift to the *Americanos*."

At Fort Bowie, life went on as usual. Captain Vincent Parmalee, Chief of Scouts, stood in front of his commanding officer's desk. "You sent for me, sir?"

Colonel Reynolds looked up from the report he was filling out. Sometimes it seemed to him that he spent half his military career doing forms and the other half riding roughshod over incompetents like the captain. "Yes, I did. At ease."

Parmalee relaxed, but not much.

"If you'll recall, I sent word to you yesterday that I wanted your best scout, that fellow Quick Killer, sent out with Captain Derrick's next patrol. Derrick is going after Delgadito and will need all the help he can get." Reynolds leaned back. "Did you receive the message?"

"Yes, sir. The orderly delivered it promptly."

"Then why the hell isn't Quick Killer here? Derrick is out there with all his men, saddled and waiting."

Captain Parmalee shriveled inside. "I know, sir. But there's a slight problem."

"How can that be? Not two weeks ago Quick Killer was standing in the very spot you are, practically demanding that I send him after Delgadito. Has he changed his mind?"

"No, sir. It's not that."

"Damn it. Then what is the problem?"

"I don't know where Quick Killer is," Parmalee admitted, trying to shrink within his uniform. "He disappeared from the fort shortly after his little talk with you and no one has seen him since."

Colonel Reynolds began drumming his fingers on the desk. "Why wasn't I informed?"

"I was hoping I would find him before this, sir," Parmalee whined. "I didn't want to bother you over a trifle."

"A trifle!" the colonel exploded, coming out of his chair. "Our best scout up and vanishes and you don't rate it news worthy of my attention?" Reynolds swept

170

around the desk and reared over the junior officer. "I've tolerated about as much of your bungling as I'm going to. I know you have a drinking problem. Hell, half the men stationed here do. But that's no excuse for gross misconduct. Didn't it occur to you that he might have gone off on his own after Delgadito?"

"Yes it did, sir," Parmalee answered, flushing with anger at the aggravation the damned breed had caused him. If and when Quick Killer did return, Parmalee was going to find a way to repay the scout in spades.

Reynolds lifted a hand as if to poke his subordinate in the chest, but then simply sighed and sat back down. "Captain, I want him found. Take as many men as you need. Scour the reservation from one end to the other if need be. But find him and bring him here before the end of the week, or so help me God I'll have you sent to a post that will make this one seem like the Ritz in New York City. Do you understand, mister?"

"Yes, sir."

"Good. Get the hell out of my sight."

Grateful for the reprieve, Parmalee scurried outdoors and hurried across the compound to his small, dingy office. He paused to glance back, and when assured no one was looking, he pulled out his flask. His hands shook as he shoved the door wide, stepped inside, and tipped the bottle to his lips. The whiskey seared his mouth, his throat, warming them and his belly as he gulped greedily. It used to be that he couldn't get through the day without a glass or two. Now he couldn't get through an hour without draining half the flask. But how dare the colonel accuse him of not being able to hold his liquor! he fumed. He did as good a job as—

Suddenly an awful stench assailed Captain Par
malee's nose. He jerked the flask down, almost gag
ging when he inhaled. Bewildered, he looked around
then felt his whiskey making the return trip.

A ghastly object rested on top of the captain's
desk, positioned in the center where it leaked ooze
and pus and gore. The flesh was discolored, the
tongue protruded, the jaw split wide, but there was
no mistaking those cruel facial features.

It was Quick Killer's head.

WHITE APACHE

Jake
McMasters

Follow Clay Taggart as he hunts the murdering S.O.B.s who left him for dead—and sends them to hell!

#1: Hangman's Knot. Strung up and left to die, Taggart is seconds away from death when he is cut down by a ragtag band of Apaches. Disappointed to find Taggart alive, the warriors debate whether to kill him immediately or to ransom him off. They are hungry enough to eat him, but they think he might be worth more on the hoof. He is. Soon the white desperado and the desperate Apaches form an alliance that will turn the Arizona desert red with blood.

___3535-9 $3.99 US/$4.99 CAN

#2: Warpath. Twelve S.O.B.s were the only reason Taggart had for living. Together with the desperate Apache warriors who'd saved him from death, he'd have his revenge. One by one, he'd hunt the yellowbellies down. One by one, he'd make them wish they'd never drawn a breath. One by one, he'd leave their guts and bones scorching under the brutal desert sun.

___3575-8 $3.99 US/$4.99 CAN

LEISURE BOOKS
ATTN: Order Department
276 5th Avenue, New York, NY 10001

Please add $1.50 for shipping and handling for the first book and $.35 for each book thereafter. PA., N.Y.S. and N.Y.C. residents, please add appropriate sales tax. No cash, stamps, or C.O.D.s! All orders shipped within 6 weeks via postal service book rate. Canadian orders require $2.00 extra postage and must be paid in U.S. dollars through a U.S. banking facility.

Name_____
Address _____
City _____ State _____ Zip _____
I have enclosed $_____in payment for the checked book(s).
Payment <u>must</u> accompany all orders.☐ Please send a free catalog.

WILDERNESS

GIANT SPECIAL EDITION:
SEASON OF THE WARRIOR

By David Thompson
Tough mountain men, proud Indians, and an America that was wild and free—authentic frontier adventure during America's Black Powder Days.

The savage, unmapped territory west of the Mississippi presents constant challenges to anyone who dares to venture into it. And when a group of English travelers journey into the Rockies, they have no defense against the fierce Indians, deadly beasts, and hostile elements. If Nate and his friend Shakespeare McNair can't save them, the young adventurers will suffer unimaginable pain before facing certain death.

_3449-2 $4.50 US/$5.50 CAN

LEISURE BOOKS
ATTN: Order Department
276 5th Avenue, New York, NY 10001

Please add $1.50 for shipping and handling for the first book and $.35 for each book thereafter. PA., N.Y.S. and N.Y.C. residents, please add appropriate sales tax. No cash, stamps, or C.O.D.s. All orders shipped within 6 weeks via postal service book rate. Canadian orders require $2.00 extra postage and must be paid in U.S. dollars through a U.S. banking facility.

Name_____
Address_____
City _____ State _____ Zip_____
I have enclosed $_____in payment for the checked book(s).
Payment <u>must</u> accompany all orders. ☐ Please send a free catalog.

Judd Cole

Follow the adventures of Touch the Sky as he searches for a world he can call his own!

#5: Blood on the Plains. When one of Touch the Sky's white friends suddenly appears, he brings with him a murderous enemy—the rivermen who employ him are really greedy land-grabbers out to steal the Indian's hunting grounds. If the young brave cannot convince his tribe that they are in danger, the swindlers will soak the ground with innocent blood.

_3441-7 $3.50 US/$4.50 CAN

#6: Comanche Raid. When a band of Comanche attack Touch the Sky's tribe, the silence of the prairie is shattered by the cries of the dead and dying. If Touch the Sky and the Cheyenne braves can't fend off the vicious war party, they will be slaughtered like the mighty beasts of the plains.

_3478-6 $3.50 US/$4.50 CAN

#7: Comancheros. When a notorious slave trader captures their women and children, Touch the Sky and his brother warriors race to save them so their glorious past won't fade into a bleak and hopeless future.

_3496-4 $3.50 US/$4.50 CAN

LEISURE BOOKS
ATTN: Order Department
276 5th Avenue, New York, NY 10001

Please add $1.50 for shipping and handling for the first book and $.35 for each book thereafter. PA., N.Y.S. and N.Y.C. residents, please add appropriate sales tax. No cash, stamps, or C.O.D.s. All orders shipped within 6 weeks via postal service book rate. Canadian orders require $2.00 extra postage and must be paid in U.S. dollars through a U.S. banking facility.

Name _____
Address _____
City _____ State _____ Zip _____
I have enclosed $_____in payment for the checked book(s).
Payment <u>must</u> accompany all orders.□ Please send a free catalog.

RED-HOT WESTERN ACTION
BY JACK SLADE!

Rapid Fire. For a handful of gold, Garrity will take on any job—no matter how many corpses he has to leave behind. And when the lone triggerman rides into a dusty cowtown, the locals head for cover. They know there are a hundred ways to kill a man on the savage frontier, and Garrity has used them all.

__3488-3 $3.99 US/$4.99 CAN

Texas Renegade. Cursed by the hard-bitten desperadoes he hunts, Garrity always gets his man. And for a few dollars more, he promises to blast the shiftless vipers terrorizing a small Texas town to hell and beyond.

__3495-6 $3.99 US/$4.99 CAN

LEISURE BOOKS
ATTN: Order Department
276 5th Avenue, New York, NY 10001

Please add $1.50 for shipping and handling for the first book and $.35 for each book thereafter. PA., N.Y.S. and N.Y.C. residents, please add appropriate sales tax. No cash, stamps, or C.O.D.s. All orders shipped within 6 weeks via postal service book rate. Canadian orders require $2.00 extra postage and must be paid in U.S. dollars through a U.S. banking facility.

Name _____
Address _____
City _____ State _____ Zip _____
I have enclosed $_____ in payment for the checked book(s).
Payment <u>must</u> accompany all orders.☐ Please send a free catalog.